# WHAT IF?

**Other books by Robert Blumetti:**

*Ironstorm*

*The Falin Crisis*

*Galactic Affairs Short Stories*

*The Return of the White Stone*

# WHAT IF?

## Alternative Historical Time Lines

### Robert Blumetti

iUniverse, Inc.

New York Lincoln Shanghai

# What If?

## Alternative Historical Time Lines

iUniverse, Inc.

For information address:
iUniverse, Inc.
2021 Pine Lake Road, Suite 100
Lincoln, NE 68512
www.iuniverse.com

ISBN: 0-595-30139-8

Printed in the United States of America

*This book is dedicated to my sister, Lettie, who always makes us feel loved and appreciated.*

# Contents

▼

*A special thanks to Rudolph Carmenaty for his assistance with the proofreading of this book.*

**Napoleon battles Indians in the Northwest Territories during the Indian Wars - 1813**

**Napoleon Bonaparte reviewing his army before the battle of nottingham, 1802**

In 1836 an aged President Bonaparte informs the Senate that he will not seek another term as President, and is prepared to retire as a private citizen. Vice-President Jackson listens from his desk on far left and Napoleon Bonaparte II is sitting, center roll, fourth from right.

# THE BATTLE OF NOTTINGHAM
## AUGUST 21, 1802

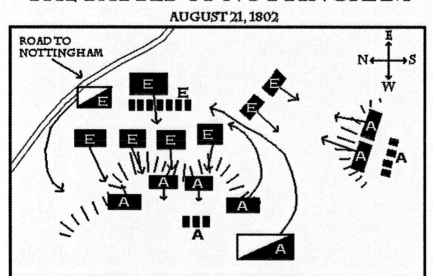

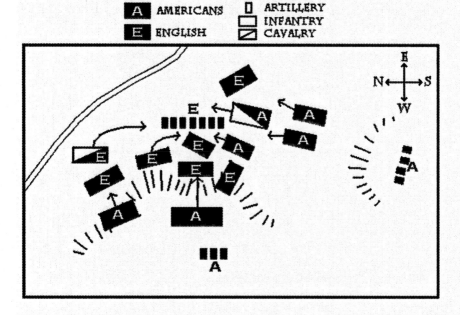

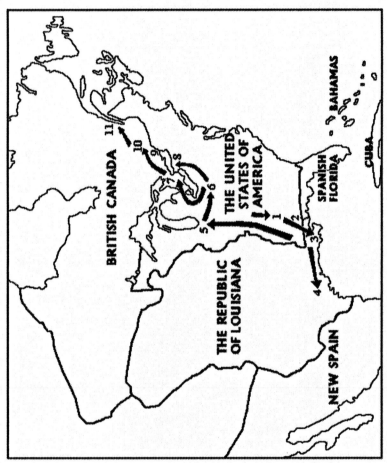

NAPOLEON'S CONQUEST OF THE NORTH
AMERICAN CONTINENT 1807-1808

1  BATTLE OF TOMBIGBEE
2  BATTLE OF FORT MIMS
3  BATTLE OF NEW ORLEANS
4  BATTLE OF GOLIAD
5  BATTLE OF FORT DEARBORN
6  BATTLE OF THREE TRIBES
7  BATTLE OF THAMES
8  BATTLE OF NIAGARA
9  BATTLE OF YORK
10 BATTLE OF MONTREAL
11 BATTLE OF QUEBEC

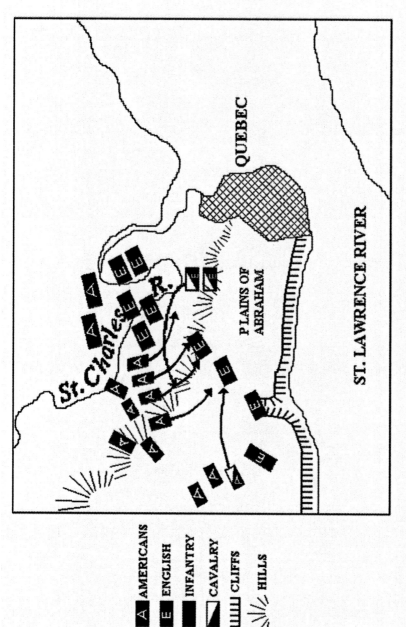

THE BATTLE OF QUEBEC 1809

CENTRAL EUROPE - 1866

CENTRAL EUROPE - 1867

# WHAT IF BISMARCK CREATED GREATER GERMANY IN 1866?

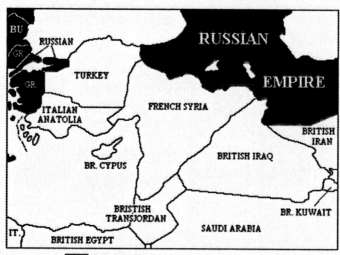

THE RUSSIAN EMPIRE AND SATELLITE STATES

# WHAT IF THE ALLIES WON WORLD WAR ONE IN 1916?

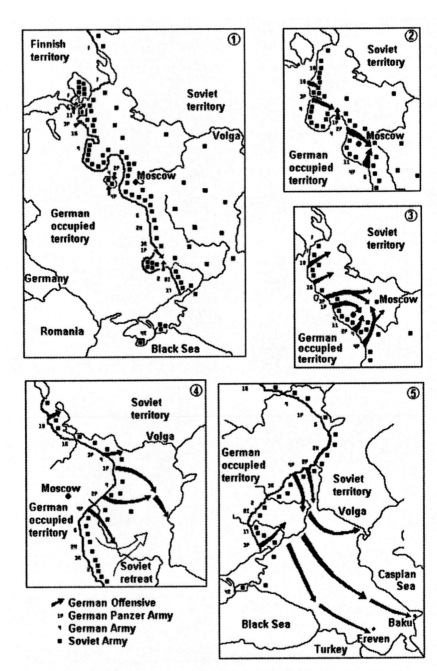

**GERMANS ATTACK MOSCOW IN 1942**

# WHAT IF NAPOLEON WAS BORN IN AMERICA?

**BY**
**ROBERT BLUMETTI**

## A DEATH AT YORKTOWN

The battle of Yorktown was fought with bravery on both sides. The Americans stormed the British lines with a zeal born out of a new nation determined to achieve its independence from their mother country—turned oppressor. Many died on both sides—Englishmen and Americans. Their blood mingled on sacred ground. But among their numbers were men not born Englishmen. Men from many countries, seeking liberty and opportunity in the New World, found themselves thrust into a conflict—one from which they did not flinch to join. Poles, Germans, Frenchmen and other nationalities fought for the American cause, all responding to the spirit of the age. Among the many foreigners who joined the ranks of Washington's army was a refugee from the island of Corsica.

Carlo Bonaparte and his wife, Letizia and son, Joseph left Corsica in March 1769, and sailed to England. But they didn't stay in England. Carlo immediately took his family and sailed for New York City. The Bonaparte family arrived in New York in June, 1769. Five weeks later Letizia gave birth to a baby boy and named him Napoleon.

The body of Carlo Bonaparte was removed from the battlefield of Yorktown by two soldiers, as Colonel Alexander Hamilton watched. Carlo first met Hamilton after he arrived in New York City. Hamilton appreciated the passion that the Corsican possessed for the cause of liberty. From the very beginning, Carlo Bonaparte sided with the Americans against the British, as revolutionary fever began to grow in the American colonies. After hostilities broke out, Carlo served Hamilton as an orderly during the Revolutionary War. He fought alongside Hamilton and Washington when the British attacked Brooklyn Heights and New York City. His wife and three sons (Lucien was born shortly after Napoleon) fled the city and took refuge with Robert Morris' family. But when Carlo left with Hamilton and Washington, he took his two oldest sons, Joseph and Napoleon with him. They served and fought loyally and bravely through the years, in New Jersey, at Valley Forge, in Pennsylvania and finally at Yorktown.

"Be proud of your father, boys," Hamilton said. "Never forget what he fought and died for. He gave his life so that a new nation could be born. No man could be a better American, even though he was born on foreign soil, he was 100 percent American."

The young Napoleon thought to himself what it meant to be "100 percent American." Hamilton was also born on foreign soil. Perhaps their foreign birth was why his father and Hamilton were able to bond. And yet they were Americans. His young, but brilliant mind, rolled over the meaning of the words. America was a new nation. What did it mean to be 100 percent American? The destiny of America was yet to be determined. The young Napoleon decided that he would make sure that his father did not die in vain. It was up to him to make sure that his father's death would have meaning. He swore that he would make sure that this new nation, would one day become the greatest nation that ever existed. Something deep within him, perhaps it was his father speaking to him from the grave, perhaps it was the goddess Fortuna, he did not know, but what he did know was that this mission was his destiny.

Hamilton placed a hand on a shoulder of each boy.

"I promised your father that if anything happened to him, I would see to your education and future occupation," Hamilton said. "You will both come and work for me. And there will be a great deal of work in the years to come."

Hamilton was as good as his word. Both Joseph and Napoleon were employed by Hamilton, helping him in his work to shape the new nation. Since Hamilton was a close confidant to George Washington, both boys worked closely with the General of the Continental Army. Napoleon was present when Washington, at Newburgh, New York, convinced his officers to remain loyal to the Republic and not try and set him up as dictator. The young Bonaparte was moved by Washington's humility. The love and admiration that his officers felt for their commander in chief was contagious, and Napoleon knew at that moment that he wished to pursue a military career.

# THE WASHINGTON ADMINISTRATION

When Washington was elected as the first President of the United States, Hamilton served as his Secretary of the Treasury. Both Bonaparte brothers, along with their younger brother, Lucien, worked under Hamilton.

Those first years were difficult ones for the young nation. Under Washington's steadfast leadership, Revolutionary America slowly evolved into a Republic. The 1790s was a decade that produced two great men, Thomas Jefferson and Alexander Hamilton. Each represented a movement that wished to fashion the new nation and its government in a distinct, ideological fashion. Hamilton favored a powerful national government and a strong union, while Jefferson supported a weak Federal Government and a broader and freer democratic system. Napoleon naturally supported Hamilton's point of view.

Napoleon Bonaparte sided with Hamilton when he set up the Bank of the United States, modeled on the Bank of England. Like his mentor, he agreed with the establishment of a national mint and tariff duties to help develop national industries. He especially supported the establishment of a strong army and navy.

One of the vexing problems Washington faced during his terms as President was the continued conflict between the Indians and white settlers, who after the Revolution, began flooding into the western territories. Most of the land was uninhabited. The settlers cleared the forests and built cabins, farms and towns. They quickly brought order to the wilderness. The Indians lived as nomads, by moving from hunting ground to hunting ground, as the seasons changed. The Indians devastated the landscape by burning forests and killing the game animals. This usually resulted in terrible and bloody wars among the many different tribes. But with the expansion of the way of life of the American settlers pushing westward, their nomadic lifestyle was threatened. Everywhere they shouted, "White man shall not plant corn north of the Ohio."

The conflict between the white settlers and the Indians grew. Washington sent an expedition of fifteen hundred militiamen from Pennsylvania and Kentucky to confront the tribe of the Miamis. Unfortunately, the commander of this small army, Arthur St. Clair, led his men into an ambush, losing over nine hundred men, and forcing him to retreat.

After reading the report, Washington put it down on his desk. He rubbed his eyes as if, trying to drive away the pain.

"First Josiah Harmar defeated in 1791 and now Arthur St. Clair was routed by the Redman," Washington said. "He lost over nine hundred good men. It's a disaster."

"We'll have to send out another troop," Hamilton said. "If we don't, the Indians will burn every settlement northwest of the Ohio River."

"I know, Alex," Washington sighed. "But who shall we pick to command the new force? We can't afford another defeat."

"Napoleon Bonaparte," Hamilton did not hesitate to volunteer his young apprentice.

"Are you sure?"

"Yes, Mr. President. Bonaparte is tough as a squirrel, possesses a brilliant mind and is able to move men to passion. If anyone can raise a force and lead them to victory, it's Napoleon."

Washington looked up at Hamilton. His stoic face was tempered by a toothless smile. He was amused by the zeal with which Hamilton praised his protege.

"He was always a brave and dedicated lad during the war," Washington remembered. "He never flinched at the clamor of battle or the sight of so much death."

"He possesses the grit of his ancestral Corsica and fearlessness forged from iron."

"That he does," Washington agreed. "Napoleon, it is." Washington wrote up a commission of the rank of colonel.

## THE LITTLE TORNADO

The Indians grew confident since their defeat of St. Clair, and their leaders encouraged further attacks on the American settlements. No settlement was safe northwest of the Ohio River. The Indians were extremely brutal, killing all men and raping and torturing the women and children. As news of the Indian attacks spread throughout America, a war clamor arose.

In spring Napoleon Bonaparte moved out from Fort Washington at Cincinnati, with a force of three thousand highly trained troops, as well as two hundred mounted Kentucky riflemen that volunteered, led by "Mad" Anthony Wayne. As he moved north, he built a chain of forts. Bonaparte spent the winter of 1793-94 at Carlville, Ohio which he named after his father. So far Napoleon Bonaparte's success had resulted largely from the good fortune of being on Hamilton's staff.

(This would later open possibilities when Hamilton joined President Washington's cabinet.) Bonaparte was blessed with being at the right place at the right moment. Though he was present at many of the battles of the Revolution, he was just a youth. This was to be his first large-scale military operation. He had studied hard and worked even harder and was confident of his abilities. Now he had the opportunity to test those abilities, to prove that he had talent as a military commander of the first rank.

He handpicked his force of three thousand regulars and drilled them relentlessly into a professional army. He studied the memoirs of Julius Caesar, his favorite reading, and applied Caesar's techniques to train his troops. He intended to use them against the Indians, much as Caesar used his troops against the barbarous Gauls. The Indians, between fifteen hundred and two thousand warriors from a half-a-dozen different tribes were out numbered by Napoleon's forces. At first they retreated to a British fort on American soil, but eventually decided to turned and fight at Fallen Timbers, a wide swath which a tornado had cut in the woods.

On August 20th, the battle began with a charge by the Kentucky cavalry against the Indian's left flank. With white horsehair plumes flying and sabers glittering, the mounted Kentuckians, led by Anthony Wayne, galloped through a fiery wall ignited by the Indians. They leaped the timber barricades and fell upon the enemy with flashing steel. The infantry moved out and began surrounding the Indians on both flanks. Once in position, they fired a volley and then charged with bayonets.

Napoleon grabbed the Stars and Stripes and charged with his men at the Indian barricades. "Colonel, you'll get yourself killed," William Henry Harrison said as he ran after Napoleon.

"Only if the Gods will it," Napoleon said.

"And they call Wayne 'Mad,'" Harrison said.

An Indian leaped at Napoleon, only to be impaled on the flagpole. Napoleon fell back and would have been killed by another Indian if not for Harrison, who cut down the red man and hauled Napoleon away. Napoleon and Harrison became close friends. Napoleon's courage inspired his men to victory.

The Indians tried to flee, but discovered too late that they were encircled by Napoleon's forces. It was over in less then thirty minutes.

Napoleon Bonaparte showed no mercy. He killed all the Indians, brutally chopping them to pieces. He spared one Indian from each tribe and sent him back to his people to warn them not to take up arms against the United States. If they did, he told them, he would cut through them with all the devastation of tornado cutting through the woods. Napoleon was good as his word and began to storm throughout the countryside, burning any Indian settlements he encountered, killing anyone who resisted. The Indians soon discovered that British assurance of support were mere words and not action. Soon all Indian resistance collapsed, and Bonaparte became known as the Little Tornado by the Indians. With Bonaparte's victory, the British were forced to withdraw from American soil.

Bonaparte's fame spread throughout the United States. He was able to test his military ideas during the war with the Indians, and was now established as the foremost military figure in America. His popularity rose. Publications began writing about his exploits on the frontier. He became famous as a great Indian fighter. He was affectionately referred to as the Little Tornado. But among those who opposed Washington, Bonaparte was referred to as, Washington's Little Caesar. Such talk was of little consequences to him. He was confident in his abilities and in his destiny.

# DEFENDER OF THE REPUBLIC

"Have you seen this article?" Hamilton asked Bonaparte. "Little Caesar! They call you a Caesar. These packs of anarchists and revolutionaries. They hate Washington because he refuses to enter the war in Europe on the side of the French Republic, and they take their frustrations out on you. They would have us declare war on all of Europe, and they call you a Caesar."

Napoleon sat and watched Hamilton pace back and forth waving the newspaper in the air. He was wiry in built and stood only five foot, two inches tall. He still wore his chestnut hair long. His face seem to shine and his grey eyes radiated with a serene confidence.

"Someday I'll prove them wrong," Bonaparte said. "If Providence would be so generous as to afford me the opportunity, I'll someday prove myself greater than Caesar."

Hamilton stood in mid-step and stared at his friend. "You're joking?"

Bonaparte smiled a half-smile. "My ambition is not to undo the work of so many who have fought and died to set up this Republic, but to expand its limits beyond what they might have hoped to be its boundaries. To build a grand federal system that will ensure its survival far into the future."

"You can start in western Pennsylvania," Hamilton said. "There is talk of rebellion and the talk has turned into acts of sedation. Are you confident in the professionalism of your troops?"

"I am," Bonaparte said. "I leave with them in the morning. After I'm finished, the rebellion will be put down."

"I hope so, Napoleon. We cannot permit rebellion to go unpunished. If we do, it will so weaken the Federal Government that it will cause the many states to go flying asunder into the abyss and put a premature end to this noble experiment we call the United States."

"Neither Fortune nor I will permit it," Napoleon said.

"I hope so," Hamilton said. "President Washington agreed with me that you were the best man for this task. There was opposition in the Congress, but we were able to raise the money to pay for the fifteen thousand troops. You must squelch the rebellion in the four western counties of Pennsylvania, and demonstrate the authority of the Federal Government. But don't be brutal."

"I understand what has to be done."

"My God go with you. The fate of the Republic lies in your hands."

Bonaparte was better than his word. He left the next morning, force-marching his troops the entire way. When he reached the rebellious counties, he decided to use tact. His army asserted its authority and arrested hundreds of malcontents, but let all but eighteen go after they singed an oath respecting the laws of the land. After he returned to Philadelphia with the arrested rebels for a trail, he spoke up for them, begging lenience. Only two were convicted and Washington quickly pardoned them. Bonaparte was now seen as a military leader with sound political sense. He was soon worshiped by most Americans, especially on the frontier.

# AN AMERICAN CAESAR

Hamilton stormed into his office. Napoleon and his two brothers, Joseph and Lucien were both present. The three young men look up from their desks. They were beginning to get used to Hamilton's stormy appearances after attending Washington's cabinet meetings. Joseph and Lucien looked at each other and then at their brother Napoleon who sat unmoved. They instantly knew that Hamilton and Jefferson had argued at the meeting.

"Damn that Jefferson! Confound and damn him!" Hamilton's fist slammed hard on his desk. He sat in his chair, red faced and wide eyes.

"You shouldn't let Jefferson get under your skin," Napoleon said. "You're going to bust a blood vessel. Then we'll have to clean up all the blood."

Hamilton looked at the young man and laughed. Napoleon could say the most ridiculous things with the most serious face. It wasn't that he had a developed sense of humor, because he was almost always serious. But he always managed to say something to cause Hamilton's temper to wane and recover from his fits of anger after arguing with Jefferson.

Hamilton shook his head and smiled.

"What was the argument about?" Napoleon asked.

Hamilton took a breath and released all his tensions.

"France," he said. "What else? That fool, Jefferson wants us to go to war against all of Europe. He wants us to honor the 1778 treaty and fight for those butchers in Paris. For the last seven years he has opposed the construction of a navy and the building of a strong army, and now he seeks to plunge us into a war with the greatest powers in Europe. I'm just as outraged over British impressment of our seamen, but damn it, we have no warships worth mentioning that can take on the British navy. If Jefferson and his crowd hadn't opposed my plans to transform America into a military power, we could effectively defend our sovereignty on the high seas and on land."

"What did the President decide?" Napoleon asked.

"He ordered Jefferson to send a communicate to the British ambassador demanding the cessation of impressment and he requested John Jay go to London and negotiate a treaty. Washington does not want war, either with England or France. Thank goodness for his cool head."

"Jay is a good man and an able diplomat," Napoleon said.

"He is, and Washington is confident that he will succeed. The President always knows how to keep his head in the worst of times."

"He's a true Roman," Napoleon said.

Hamilton laughed once more. "Always the Romans. I should never have insisted your read Plutarch's Nine Lives."

"I owe you for enlightening me on the glory that was Rome. Rome was the greatest Republic," Napoleon said. "And America is the Rome of our era."

"Yes, but we don't need a Caesar."

"No, but we should seek a Cincinnatus," Napoleon said. "Now there was a true Roman. He worked all day on his farm, and living in a dirt-floor, one-room house. When he was called to save Rome, he was made a dictator. After the crisis passed, he gave up his power and returned to his little farm. Washington is like Cincinnatus. He doesn't abuse his power. Washington, like Cincinnatus, provides an example that America could learn much from."

Hamilton sat, examining Napoleon. The small frame, large head and brewing eyes. He could see greatness in the "Little Tornado." There was no task too small or too great for him. His mind was sharp and he remembered everything, word for word. But there was something else. He possessed a natural ability for leadership, it emanated with a charisma that most could not resist. He already earned a reputation in Philadelphia as the most able man in the city. Hamilton wondered if Napoleon truly was more like Cincinnatus than Caesar?

"The President is determined to avoid war," Hamilton said. "The Congress and the country are split. Jefferson's supporters cheer every battle the French armies win in Europe. They're clambering for us to declare war on Britain, as repayment for French assistance against Britain during our War of Independence."

"Won't it be advantageous for us to declare war on Britain?" Joseph asked. "We can invade and annex Canada."

"Haven't you been paying attention?" Napoleon interjected, before Hamilton could say anything. "We have no army. Before the United States can declare war on anyone, we need to build an army strong enough to see the war to a victorious conclusion. A standing army of twenty thousand in peace time, with the ability to rapidly expand to fifty thousand after war is declared. But an army by itself is not enough. The Federal Government must be charged with the duty to build a network of roads that can be used for commerce in peace, and to rapidly transfer our armies when we are at war. A country as large as our United States needs such a transportation network."

"Most people think the French are going to win the war," Lucien said. "General Jean-Baptiste Jourdan conquered the United Provinces, and compelled the British to evacuate the continent. Prussia has made peace with France, and Spain has just dropped out of the war. Austria stands alone. The revolutionary spirit is spilling into Italy and Germany. The monarchies are panicking. They fear the spirit of revolution might consume them."

"The monarchies don't understand the new spirit sweeping across the face of Europe," Napoleon said. "The days of professional, mercenary armies have passed into history. The ranks of the French armies are filled with citizen-soldiers in the tradition of the Roman Republic. We should take note and organize our own armies accordingly."

"And how would you achieve this?" Hamilton asked.

"The Federal Government should create a Military Staff. Its function should be to maintain an apparatus that can quickly and efficiently execute to victorious conclusion to any war that is thrust upon America."

"Then you are for a permanent standing army?" Hamilton asked.

"Most certainly," Napoleon said. "It's over one thousand miles from New England to Georgia. With such an exposed coast we need the means for the rapid transport of our armies, as well as a large navy."

"And who would such a army and navy protect us from?" Hamilton asked.

"Britain, of course, Napoleon said.

"You agree with Jefferson? You want to go to war on the side of France?"

"The United States must never go to war unless our interests are threatened," Napoleon said. "Since Britain controls the Atlantic Ocean, it stands to reason that the greatest threat to our territorial integrity comes from Britain. A secondary threat lies to our southwest."

"From Spain?" asked Hamilton.

"Correct. I do not advocate war, or an alliance with either Britain or France, but simply recognize that the nations whose interests most likely conflict with our interests, are Britain and Spain in that order."

"And what are those interests?" Hamilton studied Napoleon very carefully as he spoke.

"First, to maintain freedom of movement on the Atlantic ocean. Our commerce depends on it. Second, continental expansion."

"Continental expansion, what for?" Lucien asked. "We already control a vast quantity of unsettled land."

Hamilton continued to watch Napoleon.

"The North American continent is a vacuum waiting for a civilization to plant itself upon it. Where savages and wilderness now dominate, American settlers must advance our frontiers until the entire continent is incorporated into the United States. It is our manifest destiny to unite this entire continent within our Republic. And if we don't leap at the opportunity, then other nations will fill this vacuum with their own civilizations boxing us in and strangling any future growth."

Hamilton swallowed. He believed Napoleon had answered his question. He was neither a Cincinnatus or Caesar, but more like an Alexander the Great.

"I don't know if the destiny of this country is to absorb the entire continent," Hamilton said. "My immediate concern is the survival of the United States, and my own well being."

"You still intend to resign your position and return to New York City?" Napoleon asked.

"Yes, I do."

The three Bonaparte brothers exchanged glances.

"Then we will return with you," Napoleon said.

"But your star is rising here. Why would you leave?" Hamilton asked.

"Washington will not run for a third term. And I do not believe the Federalists will elect one of their own to the presidency next year."

"You don't expect Vice-president John Adams to replace Washington?"

"No. I fear Jefferson will become President," Napoleon said. "And we will find ourselves at war with Britain. That is why I want to return with you to New York. I need to cultivate friends of influence, so that I can procure a military commission in a Republican government if war breaks out. I can't do that here if Jefferson is President."

Hamilton nodded. He couldn't argue with Napoleon's logic.

"Then you will all return to New York City with me," Hamilton said. "I'm sure your mother and sister will be pleased to see you all once more."

# PRESIDENT JEFFERSON

In Europe the French armies were victorious against the Second Coalition. General Jourdan drove the British out of the Netherlands and crossed the Rhine. General Moreau defeated the Austrians in southern Germany. Lazare Carnot, known as the Organizer of Victory in France made plans for the French armies to march on Vienna. President Washington steered the United States on a neutral course. He maintained peace, but satisfied no one. The Republicans led by Jefferson were planning to run Jefferson for President after Washington stepped down. When Washington retired in 1797, Hamilton wrote his farewell speech. It called for avoiding entangling alliances and going to war only if America's interests are threatened. The Federalists rallied behind John Adams. When the results were counted, Jefferson came in first. Adams lost by one vote, but he refused to remain on as Vice-president and withdrew from the race. His votes were split and would have gone to Aaron Burr, who came in third. Hamilton used his influence to convince enough delegates to support Jefferson as the lesser of two evils. In the end, Jefferson was elected President and Thomas Pinckney, a Federalist became Vice-president.

During Jefferson's first four years he worked hard to transform the Presidency, court etiquette was pruned, titles of honor abandoned and all aristocratic trappings abolished. He encouraged westward settlements, liberal immigration laws, and leaned in favor of France. Because of his sympathies for France, relations between the United States and Great Britain soured during Jefferson's first term.

During these years Napoleon Bonaparte courted the elite of New York and New Jersey. He was greeted as a hero by everyone, rich and poor. Napoleon was often invited to the homes of such powerful families as the Schuylers, the Livingstons and Morrises and quickly endeared himself to them. He met a young daughter of the prestigious Livingston family, Elisabeth, and fell deeply in love. They married in 1799. He was thirty and she was twenty-one and very wealthy. Now that he was well connected, he threw himself into politics in 1800, assisting Hamilton.

Jefferson was easily reelected to the Presidency in 1800. Relations with Britain continued to deteriorate. Republican mobs were agitated by French agents, who extolled the "virtues" of the French Republic and the "barbarism" of the British. The English continued to stop American ships and impress American sailors, and confiscated contraband they claimed was headed for French ports.

War fever increased throughout 1801, especially along the frontier: the Great Lakes territories and the Mississippi River. The British were stirring up the Indians against white settlers once more and Southerners were calling for the annexation of Florida, (which belonged to Britain's ally, Spain). The Southerners were also interested in selling cotton and tobacco to France and her continental allies. New Englanders opposed war with Britain and they often talked of secession if the United States declared war.

In 1801, the Federal Government moved to the new capital, Washington, on the Potomac River. Debate within the Congress on whether or not to declare war went on for days. At the impasse, President Jefferson promised to appear before Congress and ask for a declaration of war. Napoleon Bonaparte was present in Congress listening to the debates with his friend, Andrew Jackson, a representative from Tennessee. He felt that war with Britain was a foolish undertaking because the United States was unprepared. It had no army or navy worth speaking of, and if war broke out, he knew America couldn't fulfill the demands of those "Warhawks," who were calling for the invasion of Canada. They waited for President Jefferson to appear.

When Jefferson finally arrived, he stood before the assembled Congress and declared: "Gentlemen. A British frigate of fifty-two guns, *The Undaunted*, intercepted our ship, *The USS Liberty* and demanded the return of five sailors that the British captain claimed were British subjects. When our Captain James refused the British demands, the British opened fire and sank *The Liberty!*"

Congressmen erupted with shouts and hands pound on desks.

"Five Americans are dead, sixteen others are wounded, some seriously. The British executed the five American sailors they claimed were British and imprisoned the rest, including Captain James and his officers.

"God knows that I am not a man of war, but there is just so much, a man can swallow. How much longer must America bend before British tyranny? How much longer must we stand by while the King's agents stir up the Redman and slaughter our people in the west? How can we stand by as American blood is spilled into the waters of the Atlantic? If we don't act and teach the King that we have won our independence and nationhood, he will arrogantly take them away from us. Is this what this Congress wants?"

Jefferson stood tall and straight. His head was held high, as if he was addressing a higher power than the U.S. Congress. Silence floated in the hall for a second or two, before thunderous shouts of war erupted.

"Well that's done," Bonaparte said. He turned to Jackson, who was now at his side. The two men were a comical sight in Washington. Napoleon stood five feet and five inches tall, while Jackson towered at six feet and six inches. "You look pleased, Andie? You have your war."

Jackson's angular face flashed into a frightening grin. His blue eyes sparkled under the crowned of up right, wiry red hair.

"You're damn right I am, Nappy," Jackson beamed. "This is going to be a walk. We'll drive the English lobster-backs out of the Western territories and show those red savages what happens to them when they cause white blood to flow."

Bonaparte shook his head at his friend's enthusiasm. Jefferson was no coward, or a fool. But Jefferson never fought in battle. He was ignorant to what it would take to wage war. Bonaparte worked alongside Hamilton and Washington as a boy, throughout the War for Independence. He put down the Indian rebellions in the Ohio territory and later suppressed the "Whiskey Rebellion" in Western Pennsylvania. Unlike most young men, he never wasted time frolicking with the usual dalliances men of his age engaged in. He spent most of his free time growing up studying mathematics, reading the exploits of Caesar, and studying the campaigns of both Frederick the Great and Alexander the Great. His mind was encyclopedic. Instantly, he could call up whatever he read and repeat it verbatim. His experiences in war were equal to or more than any man alive.

"Your Mr. Hamilton lost," Jackson said. "I warned you you were barking up the wrong tree. Now I'm sure to get a commission in the army. I'm itching to fight the British and their Indian allies. I know I can kick their arses."

"I'm sure you will, but with what? We have no army worth mentioning."

"Don't worry about me. I'll get-together the finest lads from Tennessee and whip them into shape. I want to fight on the frontier. Give me good Kentucky horsemen and Tennessee sharpshooters and I'll drive both the red backs and the red skins out of the territories. How about you, Nappy? Are you going to try and get yourself a commission?"

"I don't rightly know, but I certainly am going to try."

"Good for you. But if you can't you're always welcome to sign up with me."

"Thank you, Andie," Napoleon Bonaparte sighed.

# JEFFERSON'S WAR

Just as Andrew Jackson predicted, he was made a general. He was sent to Tennessee and ordered to raise an army on his own. He had no trouble recruiting and soon commanded a force of two thousand men.

Hamilton did everything he could for the young Bonaparte. Hamilton's wife, a Schuyler and Napoleon's wife, a Livingston, both used their family connections and finally obtain a commission as general for Napoleon. There really was no way the Republicans could prevent Napoleon Bonaparte, the hero of the Indian wars of the 1790s, from receiving a commission. But they were shrewd enough to use his fame to prevent him from being part of one of the three poorly trained and outfitted armies that would invade Canada. Instead, they gave him the unenviable task of protecting the new capital of Washington City. His enemies thought they had outfoxed Hamilton and Napoleon's supporters. The war would be over shortly. Everyone was confident that Canada would fall within six months. And, there would be no glory for Napoleon Bonaparte and the Federalists.

Napoleon Bonaparte set about the task given him. The first thing he did was give commissions to his brothers, Joseph and Lucien, as colonels. Both had been elected to the House of Representatives and so they were able to help their brother acquire sufficient funds to put together an army of only four thousand troops. Next he sought out his officers and non-commission officers. He was particular in whom he recruited and turned down eight men for every one he accepted. He was just as particular about his soldiers. He took advantage of his orders to raise and organize an army to defend the new capital by training a citizen army en masse. After nine months of carefully picking the right men, he had a force of thirteen thousand soldiers, including calvary and grenadiers.

Next he began drilling his men until they dropped. His discipline was strict, but he always joined his men when drilling, suffering the same hardships as they did. He ate the same food, slept in the same type of pup tent, and was always talking to the men, listening to their complaints and trying to fulfill his promises, even if it meant taking money out of his own pocket. Within a year he had the finest army on the North American continent.

Things were going badly for the United States. In the first year, all three invasions of Canada were turned back in defeat. New England almost seceded. The British fleet began attacking American ships at sea, and though there was some heroic victories on the Atlantic, the United States Navy was quickly losing the naval war to attrition. The only good news was from the frontier. General Jackson's Frontier Fighters, as they were called, had beaten the Indians all along the Ohio and Wabash River. One of the young Indian chiefs that Jackson caught and executed was Tecumseh.

General Napoleon Bonaparte spent his time assembling his army outside Washington. He studied reports on the battles that were taking place in Europe between the French Republican armies and the rest of Europe. He especially found interesting the French innovation of attacking in column as oppose to attacking in line, which was the traditional means of attack. American armies were trained on the march and composed mostly of undisciplined militiamen who joined to fight and then disappear. They proved to be unreliable and unwillingly to stand their ground when under fierce attack. Bonaparte was able to submit his troops to individual training in drill and company level tactics. His soldiers took part in bi-weekly and tri-weekly battalion and division level exercise on Sundays. It included combined arms tactics, bringing forth the first time infantry, cavalry and artillery into the battlefield to learn to fight as a flexible but cohesive unit. It was this cohesion and flexibility that Napoleon hoped would give him the advantage in any battle with a large British force.

# THE HERO OF THE REPUBLIC

"Did you hear the latest news about Jackson?" Joseph asked his younger brother, as he burst into his tent. "He's routed the Indians in the Indiana Territories and forced their surrender. All the tribes east of the Mississippi River and north of the Ohio River have abandoned the British."

Napoleon didn't look up. He continued to write his reports. "I heard about Andie's marvelous victory this morning."

"I should have known," Joseph said as he sat down. "Your ability to know everything that happens before anyone else is uncanny."

Napoleon put down his quil pen and looked at his brother, sat back and smiled.

"What kind of commander would I be if I didn't make it my business to know what happens in my camp before anyone else?"

Joseph laughed and leaned forward, conspiratorially.

"Have you heard from the Congress? Did they approve your request to transfer to the North?"

"No. And I don't expect to hear from Congress," Napoleon sighed. "I've sent in those reports as a formality. I know my destiny lies here. What that destiny is, only Fate knows. She guards her secret well. I can feel it in every bone in my body. I will not be cheated, brother. You can be sure of that."

Joseph knew that tone in his brother's voice. He sat back and felt the dejection that his brother refused to admit, plagued him.

"I don't know how you can stay so calm? Those bastards in the Congress are deliberately exiling you here. There's a conspiracy to keep you from the fighting. It's deliberate and dastardly and we are going to lose the war because of it."

Napoleon chuckled with amusement at his brother's anger over his misfortune.

"Don't let it bother you. You know it's impossible to contain a 'tornado,' even one as little as myself. All the scoundrels in Babylon can't upset the plans of the Goddess of Fortune."

An orderly entered Napoleon's tent. He snapped to attention and saluted. He was out of breath, and showed signs of just having traveled a great distance in a hurry.

"Private Rogers reporting, sir. I have a message from Captain Wolf in Nottingham. The British have landed near Benedict on the Potuxent River."

Joseph stood up and accepted the dispatch and handed it to Napoleon, dismissing the orderly.

Napoleon read the dispatch. His expression didn't change. When he was finished, he looked up and smoothly smiled.

"The British have landed and are marching towards the capital. I told you Fate would not abandon me."

Napoleon Bonaparte's army was on the march to meet the British in one hour. He had trained his men well and they were moving at a fast pace, for a long distance without stopping. Napoleon had addressed them before they left, quickly and to the point. In his short speech, he made everyone understand that the fate of the new capital depended on them.

"Men! King George's redcoats have landed on American soil. Right now they are marching on Washington with fire and lead. Shall we let them pass?"

A deafening roar of No! emanated from the regiment.

"Shall we meet them with a little surprise?"

"Yes!" was the reply.

"Shall you drive the redcoats from out soil?"

"Yes! Yes! Yes!"

The British sailed into the Chesapeake Bay with four ships of the line, twenty-one frigates and more than forty-eight transports carrying twenty-one thousand troops. Admiral Nelson commanded the fleet, and Sir Harry Burrard commanded the troops.

The British ships sailed up the Potuxent River and set ashore at the town of Benedict on August 19. The local people fled before the arriving British troops. Burrard commanded 19,000 troops, including one hundred cannons and a cavalry force of two thousand. The British army was formed into a column and began marching north towards Washington.

General Bonaparte was marching to meet the British with an army of 13,000, which included a cavalry force of 1,500. But Bonaparte also possessed an artillery force of ninety-six cannons organized into twelve batteries of eight cannons apiece. Bonaparte struggled hard to raise such a large force of cannons. He had come to believe that artillery was the most important component of the army, and he intended to rely upon it heavily. He divided his artillery into batteries, which was an innovation that he hoped would give him greater flexibility on the battlefield.

The American infantry was divided into companies of two hundred men each. Four companies made up a regiment, and a brigade included two regiments, plus artillery and cavalry. His cavalry was divided into cavalry regiments of 116 horsemen.

"We have to reach Nottingham before the British," General Bonaparte said. "I know a place that will be ideal to confront the British. Half the battle won, is being able to choose the location of your choice."

"What is the other half?" Joseph Bonaparte asked.

"Personal leadership, coupled with appeals to inspire men to fight. It enhances the morale of the army by more than half in battle."

"Your men love you. They refer to you as the Little Tornado behind your back."

Napoleon looked sides way at Joseph and chuckled. "Than my men are not Republicans. They call me other things."

"If you stop the British, even the Republicans will be calling you the Little Tornado."

"More out of fear that I will overrun them, than as their savior," Napoleon laughed out loud. "But first, I have to win."

Soon the American army was just to the north of Nottingham. American scouts reported to General Bonaparte that the British were just five miles to the south.

"They're taking their sweet time," Napoleon said. "Burrard doesn't have a high opinion of us."

"Reliable British arrogance," Joseph said. "They still consider us their lost colonies."

"Well, let's see if we can deliver a lesson to King George's gentlemen that they won't long forget."

Napoleon quickly moved his army into place. He set up his main force on a large hill, facing south. The British would have to pass through him to reach the capital. Before the hill was a wide field, in which a small stream passed through it. The stream was only a foot deep, but tended to overflow. This made the field wet and muddy. Napoleon placed three brigades on this hill, with another brigade behind it in reserve along with his cavalry.

Off to Napoleon's right was another hill, but much smaller, and covered with trees. Here he placed another brigade with most of his artillery. It was far enough to the right as not to concern the British, but close enough for his artillery to fire down on them at the right moment.

"Here they come," Napoleon Bonaparte said as he looked through his telescope. "There has to be at least twenty thousand under Burrard's command."

"They out number us by a third," Joseph said.

Napoleon eyebrows rose. "Don't be concerned, brother. We have an equal number of cannons. I was right to bring along so many guns. We'll soon see how right I was."

It was late in the morning. The British quickly moved into place and were waiting. It was the American cannons that spoke first. A small detachment of cannons that were stationed on the main hill opened fire at the British. The British cannons returned fire.

General Bonaparte ordered the entire brigade to move down the hill towards the British. The formation of blue-jacketed soldiers marched with a professionalism that surprised the British. They continued to fire at the approaching Americans, but they did not break ranks. Finally the British center moved forward to meet the much smaller force of American infantry. They marched forward on courageously, cross-belts forming a white X on scarlet jackets for American sharpshooters to aim at.

Instantly, the Americans withdrew back up the hill, drawing the British up and after them. Slowly, the two flanking brigades had moved forward on either side of the approaching British as the American center turned once more and confronted the enemy on the top of the hill.

"Fire!"

American guns now unleashed their fire at the approaching British.

"Fire!"

A second volley of fire ripped into the larger force marching up the hill. Napoleon's troops were well-trained and their discipline served them well. No one lost nerve as they continued to fire into the red tide. Their ranks didn't break and their fire was fast and rapid. The British found it difficult to move forward. Their boots weighted down with mud from the wet fields. Again and again American fire cut through their ranks, until the side of the hill was covered with red jackets.

"Now. I want the reserves to begin moving to the right," Napoleon said. "Order my cannons to open fire on the British flank. I want them to blast a hole into their rear."

Just as Napoleon ordered, his cannons began pounding the British rear with everything they had. Soon smoke spoiled the British view. American cannons continued to send scything fire into the British ranks. The American cavalry, supported by the infantry reserves, moving in column formation, swept through the hole in the British line.

"Yes." Napoleon said as he continued to study the battle unfolding before him. "Our reserves have cut the British force in half. Order our left wing to move forward and drive the main British force back down the hill into our waiting right wing."

The order to move forward went out. The American ranks were now able to push down on the surrounded British. Scarlet coats laid crumpled on the sloops of the hill. The position of Napoleon's troops gave them the edge to push back the superior numbers of redcoats. The British were now trapped. Their supply line was cut. The white flag was hauled. The British army was decimated. Of the 20,000 troops, 17,500 were killed, while the American suffered 715 dead. Napoleon's victory was complete and overwhelming. In one battle, he had destroyed a superior force so completely that the Sir Burrard surrendered on behalf of Great Britain. Single-handedly, Napoleon had won the war—a war that America, was losing.

When General Bonaparte and his army returned to Washington, he was welcomed by the people. News of his victory spread throughout the nation. The city was packed with citizens seeking to get a glimpse of the victor of the Battle of Nottingham. Napoleon decided to hold a triumphal march. Outside the city he walked among his troops and received a great ovation. They formed a column and marched behind him, carrying the banners of the British Empire that they captured in battle. As they marched through the city in a torchlight parade, they were cheered by the crowds that had gathered. President Thomas Jefferson was waiting for General Bonaparte at the Presidential residence. With him were Alexander Hamilton, and the members of Jefferson's cabinet. The Justices of the Supreme Court and the leaders of both houses of Congress were also present. Even the Republican opposition to Hamilton and Bonaparte turned out to greet him as the savior of the country.

A wave of enthusiasm swept the American republic. News of Napoleon's victory and the British surrender elevated Napoleon Bonaparte to the status of a national hero, eclipsing Jackson and Jefferson. The British had never suffered such an overwhelming defeat, and the Americans had never won such a decisive victory. Victory celebrations were held in every state and Napoleon Bonaparte's march through Washington was later duplicated in Baltimore, Philadelphia, New York City and Boston to cheers and jubilation by the citizenry.

The treaty that Britain and America signed did not change the boundaries of the United States. Jefferson said the nation did not enter the war for territorial gains, but to reestablish its sovereign rights. The treaty reassured American territorial integrity, guaranteed American trading rights through New Orleans, the withdrawal of all British troops from U.S. territories, the cessation of British support for Indians, and the promise by the British to cease impressing American sailors on the high seas. Not everyone was happy with the treaty. Many wanted new territories. Jefferson' popularity dropped as did the support for the Republicans.

In Europe the armies of the French Republic were defeated in Italy and Germany in 1801. The French armies were forced to retreat to the French border, but before the armies of the Second Coalition could cross into France, General Moreau was able to appeal to the patriotism of the French people. New armies were raised before France could be invaded. In Russia, Alexander overthrew his father and was crowned Czar of Russia. He pulled Russia out of the Second Coalition. Tallyrand negotiated a peace with Europe in 1804.

# PRESIDENT BONAPARTE

Napoleon Bonaparte's popularity rose throughout the United States. President Jefferson decided not to run for a third term. After all, Washington only served two terms, and if two terms were good enough for Washington, it was good enough for him. Aaron Burr ran for the Presidency once more, but when the votes were counted, it was clear that Bonaparte captured the electorate in every state. He received 80 percent of the popular vote and 90 percent of the delegates to the electoral college.

"Congratulations, Napoleon," Hamilton said. "Your star has risen and it out-shines all others in the political sky, including us Revolutionary warriors."

Napoleon flashed a soft smile. His eyes shined and he stood with his right hand tucked inside his jacket, mocking the Roman pose of holding one's arm horizontally in front with the toga folded over it.

"Water seeks its level," he said. "I didn't seek the Presidency, it was thrust upon me by the Goddess of Fortune."

Hamilton examined his former pupil. He now wore his hair short and had gain weight. "Oh, you sought the Presidency, Napoleon. You're forgetting who you're speaking to. Always the Roman," Hamilton smiled. "You are even posing like a Roman."

Napoleon raised one eyebrow and smiled. His brothers, Joseph and Lucien and Andrew Jackson were all present. They listened to the conversation with interest. Napoleon remained unmoved by Hamilton's words.

"No man can escape his destiny," Napoleon said. "I didn't seek the Presidency because I knew it would be handed to me." He glanced at his brothers and friend. "But now that I am President, I want you to be in my cabinet."

Hamilton was taken back. Napoleon's generous offer was unexpected. He thought he understood the little man. If their positions were reversed, if Napoleon had been his mentor and he was President, he didn't think he would offer a position in his cabinet to his former mentor. He realized for the first time that Napoleon's self-confidence was real. It was neither arrogance nor a pretense. He could not be helped but be seduced by the man's certainty in his own abilities.

"In what capacity?"

"You may take your choice between the Treasury or War Department, though I wish you would choice the former."

"Why?"

"I want to resurrect the Bank of United States, and who better to offer the job to then the man who created the first one?"

Hamilton swallowed hard. The tone of Napoleon's voice was sweet with hon-est conviction. Napoleon's hypnotic personality could enthrall the soul of most men and women. "The Treasury," he finally said.

"Wonderful," Napoleon said and suddenly grabbed Hamilton's right hand with both of his. His face now blossomed in a smile so seductive that all of Hamilton's resentment vanished, healing his wounded pride.

"Then the War Department will go to Andrew. Do you agree?"

"Yes. Gladly," Andrew Jackson said.

"You and I are of like mind concerning the need for officers who will fight and instill strict discipline in our soldiers. Compulsory military service is not acceptable by the people, but we can offer incentives that will encourage young men to join the army. Free land after a period of service."

"Just as the Romans did?" Hamilton asked.

"Yes. After ten years in the service, the government will provide three hundred acres of land in the West. And we will reserve the best land for our troops. The army will be an instrument to mold the population through military service and drill. Perhaps, in time, we will be able to institute compulsory military service for all young men. But that will have to wait.

"Joseph shall be my Secretary of State. You Lucien shall remain as Speaker of the House. I will need your support there."

"Of course, brother," Lucien said.

"Alex. What do you think of John Marshall as the Chief Justice of the Supreme Court?"

"An excellent choice," Hamilton said. "He supports a strong government and is a Bonapartist."

"Then it is done," Napoleon said.

"What about Aaron Burr?" Hamilton asked.

"He came in third behind James Madison," Napoleon said. "He did come in second in the popular vote. I understand he was furious when Madison received one more electoral vote than he did. Last I heard he has some scheme to found a settlement somewhere in the southwest. Maybe in Spanish territory. There's nothing I can do about it. The Constitution is clear about the electoral vote."

Hamilton's brows sank, causing his forehead to wrinkle in reflection. "Perhaps there is a way to change that?"

"How so?"

"With a Constitutional Amendment," Hamilton said. "In future elections, we can provide for candidate teams to run for President and Vice-president, instead of the present system?"

Napoleon nodded as he thought about Hamilton's proposal. "Yes. I like it."

## THE FEDERALIST REPUBLIC

The new Bonaparte administration was able to pass several bills in Congress that expanded the strength and powers of the Federal Government. In his inauguration adress he noted, "This country has endured eight years of Federalism, and eight years of Republicanism—What do we have to show for it? We have won a war, but lost the peace. What we need is Bonapartist nationalism." Opposition by the Jeffersonian Republicans was feeble and the bills easily passed. There was strong opposition to several tariffs by Southern states that depended on exporting their goods, but both houses of Congress were dominated by Bonapartists. The tariffs were designed to support the growth and expansion of American manufacturing industries. They were also needed to pay for projects that President Bonaparte planned. A bill for the construction of interstate highways was passed. Most important was the bill that established a large standing army of 20,000 troops and a large navy. The Army and Navy were organized within a War Department that was centrally organized under a strong the Secretary of War (Andrew Jackson), and a military staff of professional generals and admirals. This military staff was given a substantial staff apparatus. It was small, but efficient and included only the ablest officers.

President Bonaparte immediately began undoing the reforms made by Jefferson. He returned the pomp and ceremony to the office of the president establishing, and what would become known as the "Imperial Presidency." He was able to establish a small elite guard of 500 troops, consisting of hardened veterans named the Presidential Guard. They were directly under the control of the President, serving as his personal body, and traveled with him whenever he ventured outside of the capital.

President Bonaparte began extending white settlements in the West. Federal highways were constructed to promote westward expansion. They stretched throughout the northwestern and southwestern territories, as well as along the Mississippi River. Forts were established to protect the settlers against the dreaded Indians. Around these forts, cities and communities rapidly sprang up.

All Western territories were federalized. The Federal Government sold plots to people for settlement. President Bonaparte created a commission that settled whites, especially poor whites, on land for free. The settlers had to work the land and repay the government 10 percent from their profits until they paid off the cost of the land. With the support of Hamilton, President Bonaparte resurrected the Bank of United States, which he used to finance these settlements. Land was also held in trust for soldiers to claim after they served for ten years. In the Southwest, slave owners sought to extend slavery into the new territories. President Bonaparte opposed the extension of slavery. Napoleon was not sympatric to the plight of the slave. (He considered the black man to be an inferior species of man, unable to live along side the white man.) His concern was for the white yeoman farmers, which he considered the backbone of the American republic.

There was opposition in the Southern States to President Bonaparte's plans for expansion. They wanted to extend slavery westward and felt the tariffs were unfair. They also resented the expansion of the power by the Federal Government. Opposition was the strongest in South Carolina, North Carolina, and Georgia. President Bonaparte worried about the issue of slavery and feared it could spilt the nation.

"Have you seen the latest reports from Europe?" Joseph asked his brother.

President Bonaparte was in his office. He stalked about with his hand in his jacket. There were four secretaries present, each taking down what he dictated. He possessed the amazing ability to dictate to four secretaries simultaneously on different subjects. Napoleon drove his staff hard, but he drove himself even harder. He would turn in at 8:00 in the evening and sleep until midnight. Then he would rise and begin reviewing the stacks of letters and reports that covered his desk. As he read, he would scribble in minutes in the margin and then left them for his secretaries to rewrite for his signature. By six in the morning he would dress and have his breakfast. Then the hard work of the day would begin, conducting meetings with his staff and cabinet, meeting with Senators, Congressmen, and other visitors. He made it a policy never to turn away anyone who came to see him, even the poorest farmer or beggar. Napoleon stopped dictating and turned to his brother. His gaze was fixed. He didn't smile and appeared wrapped in a fierce gloom.

"Yes. I read them earlier," Napoleon said. "The French are mobilizing their armies. The British have been busy forging a new coalition that includes Austria, Spain, Prussia and Russia. They have never accepted the death of the French monarchy. It was salt in the womb we opened up when we rebelled. King George can't accept two republics in one lifetime."

"Do you think they will be successful?" Joseph asked.

"Yes. I read your reports on the situation within the French government. President Moreau has made too many enemies. With the fall of Tallyrand, and flight of General Jourdan to Russia, the French government is doomed. It will hold out for three years, maybe four, but no more."

"Will they partition France?"

"No. They will restore the Bourdon dynasty, and the leaders of the Republic will be arrested and executed, if they don't get away."

"Where will they go if they escape?" asked Joseph.

"Most likely here," Napoleon said. "But if they set foot on American property, I'll have them all arrested. They're all bloody butchers. I'll never forget the way they guillotined Lafayette. He was a noble man who could have created a stable and humane government in France, but instead, they sent him to the bloody guillotine."

"At least the wars in Europe will cease."

Napoleon fixed his gaze on his brother. The fire in his eyes caused him to step back.

"That's what worries me," Napoleon said. "With France subdued, we can expect the British, with their ally, Spain, to turn on us. I fear war is on the horizon, and that's why I'm going to ask the Congress to double the size of the army and increase the number of ships in our navy."

"You'll have to call for new tariffs," Joseph said. "That won't please the Southern states."

"I know, but it can't be helped. If war breaks out, we have to be prepared. And I don't expect to wait until the British attack."

"What do you have in mind?" Joseph asked.

"It is better to kill the viper before it strikes."

# PREPARATIONS FOR WAR

In the next year President's Bonaparte's predictions were coming true. As the war in Europe progressed, the British began harassing American ships, and inciting the Indian tribes in the Northwest Territories against the white settlers. In the Southwest Territories, Spain harassed Americans at the port of New Orleans, which virtually put an end to commerce along the Mississippi River.

As relations with Britain and Spain grew worse the Congress passed Bonaparte's proposals for additional tariffs to pay for the increase in the size of the army and navy. Southern plantation owners were not pleased because of their dependency on exporting goods to England. But when the Federal Government began ordering uniforms and arms for President Bonaparte's expanded army, he purchased the goods needed from the Southern growers at top prices. This satisfied the South, but the President knew it was only a temporary solution.

President Bonaparte was also able to pass an amendment to the Constitution changing the way the Vice-president was chosen. He also passed another amendment that constitutionally established his permanent military staff under the control of the President and the Secretary of War.

# AARON BURR'S ADVENTURE

Aaron Burr never got over losing the Presidency for the second time. He began plotting new adventures and laid plans to found a state of his own. He moved to Tennessee and began organizing his own army. It was made up of frontier men and settlers. In 1805, he convinced them to join him and sail down the Mississippi River to New Orleans. Without warning he marched on the port and drove out the Spanish. Many of the French residents were veterans of the French Republican Army and joined Burr's call to form an independent state. Burr knew the Spanish would return and so he immediately set out and invaded Texas. He met a Spanish army and won a victory that established him as the ruler of most of Texas. He formed the Republic of Greater Louisiana and claimed all territories west of the Mississippi River and north of the Rio Grande, with its capital in New Orleans.

Spain raised another army in Mexico and invaded Texas. Burr sent his army to Texas and the two armies fought a battle at the missionary outpost known as the Alamo. The Spanish won, but it was a Pyrrhic victory. Burr was able to escape to New Orleans and raise another army before the Spanish were able to follow. When the Spanish eventually reached New Orleans, Burr was waiting for them. The Battle of New Orleans resulted in a Spanish victory and Burr was taken captive. He was executed by the Spanish in November, 1806.

# THE WAR WITH SPAIN

"Is there any word from the Spanish Government in the daily dispatches?" President Bonaparte asked.

"We've received no word," Hamilton said.

"Then there is no other choice," the President said. "We are at war with Spain. I want to submit a request for a declaration of war against Spain to Congress. We can't let New Orleans fall into Spanish hands once again. What is the mood in Congress, Lucien?"

"The declaration will pass."

Lucien Bonaparte was right. The Congress overwhelmingly voted for war. The Northern states supported war because commerce on the Mississippi River was threatened. The Western states wanted additional territory for expansion and hated the Spanish, who stirred up the Indian tribes against them. Indian attacks on white settlers had increased, and many suspected that both the Spanish and the British were behind the attacks. The Southern states wanted war for the same reason. Indians attacking white settlers in southern Georgia were given protection by the Spanish in Florida.

President Bonaparte was able to raise the funds for an army of 50,000, and increase the number of ships for the navy. In June 1807, Bonaparte left Washington City with an army of 30,000. He led them across the Cumberland Road to Tennessee and marched south along the Tombigbee River to Fort Mims, along with him was Andrew Jackson. In route he fought several small skirmishes with Indians friendly to the Spanish. Each time he was victorious and soon, several thousand Indians, friendly to the United States joined his army. Once in Fort Mims, Napoleon ensured that his supply lines were secure before marching on New Orleans.

Right before he left Tennessee, he received word from Vice-President Madison that Great Britain, an ally of Spain declared war on the United States, just as he expected. Madison reported that the Congress in turn, at the President's request, had declared war on Britain.

In September 1807, the American army met the Spanish army just north of New Orleans, on the eastern bank of the Mississippi River. The American forces were slightly superior to the Spanish. Napoleon sent a small part of his army forward to tempt the Spanish to attack. The Spanish took the bait and attacked. The Americans withdrew back to their fortified position that hid the bulk of the American army. Once the attention of the Spanish army was focused on the fortified positions, Napoleon suddenly unleashed his reserves and rushed them down the right flank of the Spanish forces. He used a charge by his cavalry to cover the flanking action, and cause confusion within the Spanish forces. His plan was to swing a substantial part of his army across the Spanish lines of communication and cut them off from New Orleans. The maneuver was handled by General Jackson. He was successful in encircling the Spanish army. Napoleons now sent the rest of his army forward and the two wings trapped the Spanish against the bank of the Mississippi River. The whole maneuver was over before any major engagement could be fought. The Spanish surrendered and President Bonaparte was welcomed as a hero by the citizens of New Orleans.

President Bonaparte didn't waste time in New Orleans. He stationed four thousand troops in the city and sent another thousand, with Indian allies into Florida. Once he felt his rear was secured, he immediately marched west with 25,000 troops into Texas. The Spanish sent another army of 20,000 troops into Texas. The two armies met at Goliad on the San Antonio River in October 1807. Once again the Americans overwhelmed the smaller Spanish army with a flanking maneuver. Finally the commander of the Spanish forces surrendered and agreed to yield all territory north of the Rio Grande River and the thirtieth degree latitude west, to the Gulf of California, to the United States.

# THE INVASION OF CANADA

The troops left behind in New Orleans were not negligent in their duties. They were busy constructing boats for President Bonaparte and his army to sail up the Mississippi River. Napoleon remained in New Orleans over the winter. He set to work organizing the new regions of the southwest. Roads and forts were built to protect his supplies and communications lines. When May 1808 arrived, the new territories were secured. President Bonaparte and his army set out up the Mississippi River and reached Fort Dearborn on the southern tip of Lake Michigan. He found the fort manned by troops that were under siege by the local Indian tribes. The Indians were quickly defeated and the siege lifted.

In the first week of June, Napoleon began his march across the Northwestern Territories. He split his army in two, one under his command, and the other under Jackson. The armies marched across the region, attacking any Indian tribe that resisted, and brutally destroying them. The British had been busy inciting the Indians against white settlers. These settlers considered Napoleon their savior. Napoleon was determined to put an end to Indian rebellions once and for all. He began by sending out Indian scouts loyal to him to remind the tribes of his treatment of them in 1794. Any tribe that laid down their arms would be given land to settle on after the war and become Westernized.

Few tribes accepted his offer. He was ambushed by the Shawnee, Fox and Sauk tribes. His victory was devastating. The tribes were almost entirely exterminated. The effect of his ruthless treatment caused all Indian resistance to collapse. The British were forced to withdraw from the Northwestern Territories and into Canada. But Napoleon was not going to permit them to escape. In July 1808, he invaded Canada itself from Fort Detroit.

Napoleon sent Jackson with 3,000 troops to move along the southern coast of Lake Erie. He was to rally the local militias in western Pennsylvania and western New York, and link up with General William Henry Harrison and the 2,000 troops under his command at Fort Niagara. He had defeated a British attempt to invade western New York. Captain Oliver Hazard Perry won a naval victory on Lake Erie when he destroyed a British fleet and took control of the lake. Both these events gave Napoleon Bonaparte a free hand. He marched into Canada and defeated the British at the Battle of Thames. From there, he marched to Niagara and linked up with Generals Harrison and Jackson. The American army continued its march through Canada and took the city of York after driving a much smaller British force out. The way was now open for President Bonaparte to march on Montreal. Another 4,000 troops were waiting in northern New York for Napoleon's arrival, and invaded Canada when they received news of Napoleon's siege of Montreal. After laying siege to the city, Montreal fell to the Americans in August 1808.

Napoleon pushed his soldiers hard, but they always responded to his satisfaction. The reputation he possessed among his troops was based on his personal example and deeds he performed in battle. His troops knew that he had almost been killed at the Battle of Fallen Timbers, stars and stripes in hand he lead the attack on the Indians. He always spent the night before a battle with his men, eating what they ate and suffering heat, rain or cold with them. If a bridge, wall or fort had to be built, Napoleon never failed to roll up his sleeves and pitch in, working along side the lowest private. He now took to wearing a distinctive uniform, deliberately dressing simply, contrasting with the splendid uniforms of his officers around him.

His popularity with his troops was of a special brand of love/hate. When he drove them unmercifully, they would curse him. But despite complains, the rank and file felt an affection for him that bordered on the idolatrous. He never reacted to their hostile moods or complaints, provided they performed when the occasion demanded super-human effort. A shrug of the shoulders is how he reacted and often overlooked misdemeanors and complaints. He understood the fierce independent and individualistic nature of the American people, especially among those who lived on the frontier. They might grumble and complain but they always followed him no matter the hardships.

## THE BATTLE OF QUEBEC

Napoleon Bonaparte left Montreal and marched north to the city of Quebec. With him he took 18,000 troops. The British had reinforced the city with 30,000 troops. Both sides realized that this city was the key to controlling Canada. The fall of Quebec to the British in the French and Indian War resulted in the lost of Canada by the French. Benedict Arnold's failure to take Quebec during the American War of Independence prevented the Americans from taking Canada from the British. President Bonaparte knew that he would have to take the city before the end of September when the early winter season of Canada would begin in October. If he failed, he would have to wait until next May at the earliest to try again. He was determined to win a decisive battle and force the British off the North American continent.

As Napoleon approached the city of Quebec, he used great skill to convince the British that he was worried about defeat. First he had received word that the American fleet had defeated a British fleet near Nova Scotia. The St. Lawrence River was now blocked to the British. The British could not bombard the American army before Quebec. Napoleon sent out cavalry patrols with orders to fake panic and retreat when they confront British scouts. When the American army finally arrived at the Plains of Abraham, before the city of Quebec, Napoleon presented a white flag to parley with the British. General Arthur Wellesley commanded the British forces in the city, he sent out an envoy to meet with President Bonaparte. Bonaparte went out of his way to be pleasant to the bombastic British envoy, and make them think he was trying to avoid attacking the city, and desperate for peace. With great skill he dangled the bait of an easy victory before the British. These assorted deceptions were designed to convince the British to come out of the fortified city and engage the much smaller American Army in battle. After the envoys returned to the city, Napoleon removed his army from the Plains of Abraham to its west and north along the St. Charles River.

Napoleon kept his right flank along the St. Charles under the command of General Harrison deliberately weak. A thick mist covered the plateau named the Plains of Abraham, before the city of Quebec. Wellesley felt he had the Americans at his mercy. Under the cover of the mist the British moved out of the city and occupied the Plains of Abraham. When the sun finally burned away the mist, the British could be seen by Napoleon, marching towards the lower ground. Wellesley ordered an attack on Napoleon's weakly held left flank. By nine o'clock, Harrison's troops were engaged by British troops, which crowded together on the lower reaches of the St. Charles River. Sure of success, Wellesley had practically denuded the Plains of Abraham, except for a weak detachment. The British were doing exactly what Bonaparte hoped they would do. Napoleon ordered his left wing to hold its position and delay the British right flanking movement. He then ordered the bulk of his forces in his center to attack the Plains of Abraham. The British troops on the plains were helpless before the attack. They fought bravely, but slowly they were pushed back towards Quebec. By noon, the Plains of Abraham were in the possession of the American army. Jackson, who was commanding the American attack on the Plains of Abraham, instantly turned to attack the right flank and rear of the British, who were engaged with Harrison. The British were now caught between two bodies of the

American army. They were cut off from Quebec, and their line was shattered. Soon they were panicking, and by nightfall they were fleeing in every direction.

The American victory at Quebec was complete and total with the timely arrival of the American fleet. General Wellesley surrendered. President Bonaparte was able to dictate the terms of surrender. The treaty that was drawn up at Quebec was signed and ratified by both the United States and Great Britain in December. The entire continent of North America, north of the Rio Grande and the thirtieth latitude, to the Alaskan border and the Arctic Ocean as well as Cuba, Bermuda, and the Bahamas were now part of the United States of America. President Bonaparte declared that with the Treaty of Quebec, America achieved its manifest destiny.

# THE NATIONAL PARTY

After two years of warfare, President Bonaparte was finally able to return to Washington City and perform his duties as President. Vice-president Madison welcomed Bonaparte's return with a great fanfare of parades and celebration. With a continuous flow of reports of unbroken victories, all opposition to Napoleon Bonaparte evaporated. The election of 1808 was held and Bonaparte was reelected unanimously. His brothers, Joseph and Lucien performed their duties to his satisfaction, running the campaign for their brother. Now that Napoleon was back in the capital he threw himself into his work of building a strong Federal Government.

"I want to know why progress on the construction of the new Congress building has fallen behind schedule?" Napoleon said.

"The slaves are lazy," Joseph said. "No amount of incentive can make them more industrious."

"Slaves. I wish I could purge this great nation of the blight of slavery," Napoleon said as he paced about his office. He stopped and stared at his brother. "Mark my words. I will put an end to this mark of Cain before I die."

The door to his office opened and in rushed several children.

"Papa! Papa!" the children shouted as they rushed up to the President of the United States.

Napoleon's temperament radically changed. He flung his arms about the three boys and embraced them in a collective hung and then fell over and landed on the floor to the laughter of his children. The oldest boy was Napoleon Jr. and ten years of age. Next was Carlo. He was eight. Finally, there was six years old, Joseph.

"All right, children," Napoleon laughed as the three boys climbed over him. "If you keep this up, you'll all be thrown into prison for attacking the President. That's treason, you know?"

Napoleon sat up with his legs spread wide. He watched as his wife Betsy stood in the door way with his eighteen-month-old daughter, Letizia. He reached out and smiled.

"Come to papa," he pleaded. The golden hair little girl looked up at her mother, who smiled down at her with loving eyes. She took a step forward and then, breaking free of her mother's hand she raced into her father's arms. Napoleon snatched her up and hugged her close as he kissed her on the cheek. He looked at his wife.

"I've been away too long," he said.

"You are the President," Betsy said. "You have a duty to the American people."

"But I wasn't there for little Letizia's birth."

"I understand. When I married you I knew that I was marrying a man who was destined for greatness. I saw it in you eyes. That's why I married you. I have no right to complain and you shouldn't feel guilty."

Napoleon rose and kissed his wife.

"Tell us about how you defeated the British, papa?" the boys began begging.

Napoleon surrendered to his children. With Letizia on his knee, he began telling his children of his exploits in the war against the British. This went on all afternoon until his brother departed. Napoleon loved his wife and children and never tired of doting over them.

While President Bonaparte was victorious in North America against the Spanish and the British, the French Republic was not so fortunate. The Coalition armies finally turned the tide in Europe. The French armies were defeated in Germany, Italy and the Netherlands. In the summer of 1809 the Coalition armies crossed into France and entered Paris. The French Republic collapsed and its leaders were either captured or fled. Britain, Austria, Russia, Spain and Prussia meet in Vienna and worked together to redraw the map of Europe. The Bourdon dynasty was restored in France and Louis XVIII ascended the throne in Paris.

Napoleon's war did a great deal to forge a new America nation, more mature and more independent. It knit together and strengthened its character. It renewed and reinstated the national feeling and character which the Revolution had given, and which Jefferson's war reinforced. The people no longer thought of themselves as Carolinians, Virginians, Pennsylvanians, or New Englanders. Napoleon's army gave a sense of national purpose to all the people of the Republic. His march across the face of the North American continent burnt a heightened sense of American identity into the hearts, minds and souls of the American people.

With the acquisition of such enormous territory, the growth of the Federal Government was accelerated. A strong national government was necessary to give organization to the vast, unsettled territories. President Bonaparte set about building roads to link together the vastness of the new continental empire. This helped to facilitate the settlement of the new territories, planting new towns and cities along the arteries of roads. The reorganization of the nation's economy was stimulated by the construction of a transcontinental transportation network, and tariffs were passed to protect domestic businesses and expand the American manufacturing base. A large army was maintained and a system of forts built to protect the new settlers. To protect the coast, a permanent navy was established with bases all along the entire North American coast, from Texas to Canada.

During President Bonaparte's second term many of the Republicans joined with Federalists to form a new party—the National Party. The philosophy of the new party was Bonapartism. Bonaparte's new creed combined populism with a new type of elitism, based on ability. He held a belief in political equality, economic opportunity, a hatred of aristocracy and special privileges, but also held that the successful man should be regarded as the natural leader of the nation, a strong military and support for the rise of a healthy manufacturing industry. His support for the expansion of white settlers made him a hero on the frontier. His victories against the British, and support for manufacturing and the Bank of United States generated support among the business classes. He also was popular among America's gentry because he married into one of the New York's oldest and richest families.

But there were still problems. There were resentments among the slave owners in the South, and growing tensions between the white settlers and the Indian tribes on the frontier.

## THE INDIAN WARS

By 1811 the southern frontier needed only a spark to set off an explosion of racial violence between the Indians and white settlers. Many Indians were adopting Western customs and there was some intermarriage between whites and Indians. But as the Federal Government began laying down roads and settlements on the frontier, tensions grew white hot. The Shawnee medicine man, Sekabo, related to the Creek on his mother's side, traveled south and spoke before a Creek council at Tookaubatche. He addressed five thousand Indians. He was known as the "Prophet," and told of visions from the Great Spirit and promised the Creek that they would be immune to the white man's bullets.

By spring 1812, incidents were on the rise. The efforts to peacefully assimilate the Creek lost momentum. The news of the slaughter of 247 white men, women, and children at Fort Mims, who were scalped and brutally mutilated, sent shock-waves of terror and anger echoing up and down the entire frontier. The horror of the Fort Mims massacre sparked a cry for Creek blood by Americans. President Bonaparte made plans to make war on the Creek. He assembled 20,000 regulars and 5,000 militia troops and set out with General Jackson.

President Bonaparte met with Governor Blaut of Tennessee the day before he planned to move against the Creek.

"Employ all the force you can muster and teach those barbarous sons of the woods their inferiority," the Governor said.

"I will break the power of the Creek," Napoleon said. "They had the opportunity to be assimilated into the white population. I understand many of their leaders are actually half-breeds?"

"Yes," Jackson said. "Josiah Francis, a leading Creek war hawk, is the son of David Francis, a Scotch-Irish trader. William Weatherford, who led the Creeks against Fort Mims is seven-eights white. His brother John and his half-brother David Tait lived among the Whites. His sister, Hannah McNac, raised her sons to be Creek warriors. Her husband threw in his lot with the Whites. I believe two other half-breed leaders of the Creek are Peter McQueen and Menawa."

"This will give the Creeks a slight advantage," Napoleon said. "They know much of our ways, but they lack the discipline that distinguish white soldiers from Indian warriors. Indians refuse to submit themselves to discipline. Therefore, they are not an efficient fighting force. They engage in the barbarities of savage warfare. They are doomed to destruction by their own restless and savage conduct."

President Bonaparte assembled his army near Jackson's Hermitage, and spoke before them before they departed. He took to wearing a long grey overcoat and a wide hat. He sat upon his horse, shouted with a fiery and emotional force that was deeply rooted in his temperament.

"We are about to descend upon the enemies of civilization and teach the red savages a lesson of admonition. The blood of our women and children calls for our vengeance, but must not call in vain."

A cheer rose up. The strange force that emanated from this little man was undefinable. It could engulf and seduce thousands of men and women with the ease of a smile. The term charisma is inadequate to define it.

President Bonaparte pulled on the reins of his horse and rode to his generals. "Move the army out, General."

Jackson saluted and rode off. The army began its long march south.

"I want this war terminated without delay. The swiftness of our retribution will send a chill that will strike terror into the hearts of every Indian on the North American continent," Napoleon said as he rode. He looked at Jackson. "When we are done with this business, there will be no Indian left east of the Mississippi River. Those who we do not kill will be removed to the island of Cuba. They can live along side the Negroes and mulattoes that live there."

"Does that also include those tribes north of the Ohio River?" Jackson asked.

"Yes. We will deal with them after we have dealt with the Creek and the Seminole tribes. Security is possible only once the Indian threat on our borders, and without our new, unsettled territories is finally stilled. Whites do not have to coexist with independent realities unconnected to them and beyond their control."

"What about the Indian tribes living beyond the Mississippi River?" Jackson asked.

"We will leave them for the future. This war will lay the ground plans for the methods in which those tribes will be dealt with."

On October 13, Bonaparte's army arrived at Coosa River, deep in Creek territory, and built Fort Hamilton there. The cavalry under General John Coffee, Jackson's nephew, attacked and burned the Creek village of Tallushatchee and killed everyone, even women and children. A week later, Napoleon led his troops in an attack against the main Indian army. "The Indians attacked like a cloud of Egyptian locusts, and screaming devils," Captain Davy Crockett reported.

The Indians were quickly surrounded and defeated. They were simply out maneuvered in every battle by Napoleon.

Bonaparte marched his troops fast and hard through the wilderness, sometimes retracing the same territory. When he was warned by Captain Crockett that the Indians could retake territory he had just conquered, Napoleon answered him by saying, "I may lose ground, but I shall never lose a minute. Ground we may recover, time never." Throughout the territory of the Creek warnings spread of the approach of the "Little Tornado." The American army was now far from white settlements, but Bonaparte maintained a fortified supply line with assistance from his militia troops that accompanied his army. Throughout the southwestern territories, Bonaparte's army burst upon the Creek warriors, killing and devastating them until finally, after four months of continuous fighting, the Indians agreed to surrender. Some escaped into Florida to link-up with the Seminole, but Napoleon sent Jackson after them. Jackson promised Napoleon that, "I will soon reach the promised land that flows with milk and honey, and secure it for our people and civilization." Three months later, Jackson completed the destruction of all Indian resistance in Florida.

The Indian Wars hardened Napoleon Bonaparte to the plight of the Indians. He came to view them as savages not deserving of civil consideration. From 1814 to 1829, President Bonaparte rounded up all Indians east of the Mississippi River and began the task of resettling them on the island of Cuba, which was now a United States territory. Those Indians who fought on the side of the United States were given the option to assimilate. Those who accepted were given land to farm and adopted Western customs. In two generations they disappeared into the white population through intermarriage. The northern tribes offered less resistance to removal. They were smaller and more numerous than the five southern Indian confederations, but they were less settled and never developed so large-scale an agriculture, or so completely stratified a social structure.

The removal of the Indians became the policy of how the United States would deal with other tribes as white settlements spread westward and northward across the face of the North American continent. His struggle with the Indians produced a militant egalitarianism among the American people. This sentiment grew into a strong nationalism as the Nineteenth Century progressed, and included a sentimental respect for a strong, charismatic national figure. These sentiments became the twin pillars of the new American nationalism.

Napoleon's wars with Spain and Britain, as well as his wars against the Indians generated a strong national state. He also was viewed as the tribune of the people against entrenched special interests that were the remnants of the old Republican Party. He fought conspiratorial enemies who were seeking to topple him from power. He emphasized agrarian values in planting new white settlements, and supported the growth and development of cities and new manufacturing industries at the same time. But there was yet one more crisis that President Bonaparte would have to face.

## SECESSION AND SLAVERY

Americans were anxious to purchase European goods that were superior to those produced by American manufacturers. British merchants deliberately dumped goods into America at low prices, even at a loss, to bankrupt American industry. At President Bonaparte's urging, Congress moved to prevent the death of American manufacturing by increasing tariffs to a full 30 percent. New Englanders sympathized with the bill heartily, while the South objected. Southerners wanted to keep the tariff as low as possible.

Southern states were also angered by President Bonaparte's refusal to support the extension of slavery into the new territories. He charged that, "America did not go to war against Spain, Britain and the Indian tribes so that the territories could be settled by African slaves. These new territories must be the birthrights for white settlers to settle and expand American civilization."

In 1812 the Republican Party centered in the South, fielded a candidate from Georgia, William Crawford, who opposed the tariffs and supported the extension of slavery. Many in the South, especially in South Carolina, threatened to secede from the Union if Bonaparte was reelected. Crawford's campaign was the last hurrah of the Republican Party in America. President Bonaparte easily won reelection to a third term in 1812.

In January 1813, South Carolina passed the Nullification Ordinance "to nullify certain acts of Congress of the United States, purporting to be laws, laying duties and imports on the importation of foreign commodities." The South Carolina government declared tariffs null and void in South Carolina.

"You can't just sit back and accept this act of rebellion," Joseph said.

"I'm not," President Bonaparte assured his brother. "Justice Marshall has already passed a ruling on the Nullification Ordinance, declaring it unconstitutional. If South Carolina doesn't back down, I'm going to send Andy Jackson down there with 10,000 troops and crush that den of vipers in Charleston."

President Bonaparte sent a warning to the South Carolina governor and Legislature, demanding South Carolina retract their declaration of secession and the Nullification Ordinance by February, or he would consider South Carolina in a state of secession and rebellion. When the deadline came and went, President Bonaparte declared South Carolina in a state of rebellion. He spoke before a joint secession of both houses of Congress.

"Let the dice be thrown. As Caesar crossed the Rubicon and marched on Rome, I am ordering the army and navy to mobilize, and consider South Carolina in a state of rebellion. Disunion by armed force is treason, and I declare every member of the South Carolina Executive and Legislature branches of government that voted for, and support the act of secession, to be traitors."

Bonaparte sent the army into South Carolina, led by Andrew Jackson, the most popular and best military figure after himself. The navy was ordered to blockade the coast and fire on any ship trying to leave the leave any of South Carlina's ports. Bonaparte vowed to meet what he called treason with force. The leaders of the rebellion quickly backed down as anger and outrage spread throughout the country, calling for Bonaparte to hang the traitors. The other Southern states deserted South Carolina and declared their loyalty to the United States of America.

Jackson marched through the state swiftly and with little resistance. The South Carolina militia tried to oppose Jackson, but his troops quickly dispatched them without losing a man. He made it known that only individuals who took up arms against him would be considered and treated as traitors. The people of South Carolina did nothing to resist and many hailed Jackson as a liberator. The only resistance came from the class of slave owners. Poor white farmers had been promised land to settle in the western territories and were not anxious to extend slavery westward.

Jackson soon marched into Charleston and arrests were made. Some of the traitors escaped but most of them were caught, tried, found guilty, but were pardoned by President Bonaparte. By the time Napoleon Bonaparte was sworn in as President in March, South Carolina's rebellion was crushed.

President Bonaparte abhorred slavery, but he was no friend of the African slave. South Carolina's rebellion was considered a slave owners' rebellion by most Americans. This provided President Bonaparte the opportunity to pass an amendment to the Constitution that outlawed the institution of slavery. Using his popularity, he passed another tariff, raising the tariffs to 40 percent and used the money to compensate the slave owners for the lost of their property. He then sent representatives to France, Germany and Italy, three countries that were ravaged by twenty years of war and hoped invite one million immigrants to settle in America. The response was overwhelming. Between 1814 and 1830 over five hundred thousand immigrants from Europe poured into the United States. President Bonaparte settled them in Virginia, George and in both Carolinas as tenant farmers.

The idea was suggested to him by his in-laws, the Livingstons and other Patroon families in New York. Like the Southern plantation owners, these families depended on the land for their wealth. But unlike their southern counterparts, they worked their fields with tenant farmers, not slaves. It was from their example that Napoleon was inspired to import immigrant farmers to work the Southern fields. But he was left with the problem of what to do with nine hundred thousand, freed slaves?

"If you try and make citizens out of the freed slaves, you will have a second rebellion on your hands, and this one will not be confined to South Carolina," Jackson said.

"I have no intension of forcing the social and political equality of the white and black races," Napoleon said. He paced about the room with hands grasped behind his back. "My enemies in the South are spreading rumors that I intend to make voters and jurors, or qualifying them to hold office. Some are even claiming I intend to encourage intermarriage between whites and blacks."

"They remember that you permitted some Indians to assimilate into white settlements in the southwestern territories," Alexander Hamilton said. He was now sixty-six years old. "I was born in the Caribbean and remember how terrifying the threat of Negro rebellion was. I hated slavery, and I hate it now, but I also know that the two races can never live together under the same government."

"You are not the only one who holds such an opinion," Napoleon said. He reached for a letter from his desk and handed it to Hamilton. "Thomas Jefferson shares the same sentiments. He has recommend the deportation of all slaves to some location in the Caribbean. He reminds me that the slaves of Haiti and San Domingo killed thousands of whites. The race war of 1789 in Haiti was led by mulattoes against whites. He writes that it would be impossible to try an assimilate them into the white population. And I'm of the opinion that we should resettle them in Cuba, along side our Indians."

"We might be able to settle some of them in Cuba, but most will have to go else where," Joseph Bonaparte said. "The arrival of the Indians is causing problems with the locals. If we try and import another million people, civil war and revolution will break out."

"Then where?" Napoleon asked.

"I might know someone who can help us," James Madison said. Napoleon raised his eyebrows and stared. It was his way of showing interest. "James Monroe helped organized a new organization right here in Washington a month ago. It's called the Re-colonization Society of America. And its purpose is to raise funds to repatriate all Africans in America, to a self-governing country of their own, on the coast of west Africa. They call it Liberia. They have a great deal of important people supporting them."

"I want to speak with Mr. Monroe," Napoleon said. "Invite him to a meeting."

"I will," Madison said.

"Have you decided to step down as Secretary of the Treasury?" Napoleon asked Hamilton.

"I have," Hamilton said as he shifted in his chair. "Have you picked a successor?"

"Mr. Henry Clay," Napoleon said. "He has a brilliant mind and an unique ability with figures."

"A good choice," Hamilton said. "You also have support in Congress from John Quincy Adams."

"John Adam's son," Napoleon said.

"Yes. He is both intelligent and challenging. You might keep him in mind for a future post in your cabinet."

# THE CREATION OF A NATIONAL CULTURE

Napoleon was reelected in 1816 and again in 1820. During these years he put an end to slavery with the support of the Re-colonization Society of America. James Monroe was very proficient in raising money and support among abolitionists. The country of Liberia was founded on the western coast of Africa. The capital was named Bonapartia. The first settlers landed in 1816. The slaves were replaced by immigrants from Europe. By 1830 the South was transformed from a White Anglo-Saxon and African society to an Anglo-Saxon, Latin and German society. Eventually, the immigrants from Germany and Southwest Europe assimilated with the lower class Southern whites.

Most of the southwest territories were settled by white farmers, much like the territories north of the Ohio River. These new territories were divided and admitted into the Union as the states of Franklin, Jefferson, Ohio, Transylvania, Westsylvania, Florida, Louisiana, and Michigan. One half of the American population was settled into the trans-Allegheny west. The population was highly nationalistic and strong supporters of President Bonaparte. Almost every adult white man was eligible to vote and hold office. Just about all of them had served in the army, and about one-third fought under Napoleon Bonaparte. Many of them owed the land they lived on to Napoleon. He made sure that every soldier who fought in his armies for more than ten years was granted three hundred acres of land. He was considered their savior for providing economic security and opportunity, as well as their protector by his military exploits and victories, not just against the British and Spanish, but by removing the threat of Indian attacks.

Napoleon Bonaparte worked to strengthen the power of the Federal Government by getting three additional amendments to the Constitution passed. The first one gave the President power to appoint governors of states, who in turn had to be ratified by the state legislatures. The second amendment gave the Federal

Government the power to control new territories. And the third amendment outlawed slavery. He also used the power of the Federal Government to support the nurturing of a distinct American culture. He drafted Noah Webster to create a distinctive American language by commissioning the creation of an American language dictionary, establishing standards that would make it different from the English used by the British. He also gave support to the development of the arts. He encouraged the growth of a national system of education throughout America for all children. It would take another fifty years for these efforts to bare fruit, but the seeds were planted by Napoleon Bonaparte.

Bonaparte encouraged authors like Washington Irving to write about American legends and myths, as well as biographies of American heroes like Columbus and Washington. James Fenimoore Cooper romanticized the struggle of the white man conquering and settling the American West. He glorified Bonaparte's wars against Spain and Britain, and especially his wars against the Indians. Ralph Waldo Emerson would write a powerful biography of Napoleon Bonaparte in 1851 glorifying him and permanently placing him within a holy trinity of American heroes with Columbus and Washington. George Bancroft's massive History of the United States rejoiced in the power and role of the Federal Government, proclaiming the supremacy of America and the prominence of Columbus, Washington and Bonaparte in creating the American nation. He celebrated the idea of militarism and the role the army and navy played in building the North American empire of the United States. Themes that became integral to the American world view were the wars against the Indians, militarism, the service of the common man, the opportunity of merit over class, and the celebration of the role of the great man in history.

President Bonaparte continued to get reelected in 1824, 1828 and again in 1832. These were years of good feeling. The only major party was the National Party. During these years Napoleon worked with such men as James Monroe, Henry Clay, Daniel Webster and John Quincy Adams, appointing them to different posts in his cabinet. When the South American colonies of Spain began to rebel against Spanish rule, John Quincy Adams helped President Bonaparte to formulate the Bonaparte Doctrine, which stated that the United States would not permit any non-American power to interfere in the affairs of North and South America. To back up this doctrine, the American navy soon grew into the largest and most powerful navy in the world, second only to Great Britain's navy. President Bonaparte also appointed such men as William Henry Harrison, Davy Crockett, John Coffee, and Winfield Scott to the American Military Staff.

President Bonaparte also worked hard to transform the capital of the United States, officially naming it Washington City, into a great metropolis and center of culture, economics and government. Monumental buildings were constructed along great boulevards. The city rapidly grew as industry and finance set up their headquarters in the new capital. This was helped by the active and aggressive policies of a strong Federal Government. Huge celebration was held in the capital in 1826, the fiftieth anniversary of the Declaration of Independence. One week later the entire nation was plunged into morning, after the news that John Adams, Thomas Jefferson and Alexander Hamilton, three architects of American independence, all died on July 4, 1826.

In 1832, Napoleon Bonaparte, age sixty-three, decide not to run for another term as President. Instead, he supported the election of his Vice-president, Andrew Jackson. Jackson won by a landside, and would serve three terms. In 1848 James Polk became President and also served three terms. In 1860 Abraham Lincoln would become President, and Napoleon Bonaparte Jr., as his Vice-president, and led the United States in a war against Great Britain in the Caribbean and South America.

While Europe embarked on a rush for colonies in Africa and Asia, the United States came to dominate the Western Hemisphere. Britain lost all her holdings in the Western Hemisphere, including the Falkland Islands and St. Helena is the South Atlantic to the United States in Mr. Lincoln's war. American-British rivalry remained intense in the second half of the Nineteenth Century and into the Twentieth Century. Lincoln purchased Alaska from Russia in 1867, and annexed the Sandwich Islands in 1870. Most of the islands in the Pacific Ocean fell under American control.

The United States remained free of the system of entangling alliance in Europe. Bismarck partitioned Austria and created Great Germany in 1866. He formed the Triple Alliance with the Kingdom of Hungary and Italy. The French joined into an alliance with Russia in 1892. Fearing French, Russian and American expansion, Great Britain and Japan joined the Triple Alliance with Germany in 1907. When war broke out between the two alliances in 1912, President Napoleon Bonaparte, the great, great grand son of Napoleon declared the United States neutral and the Western Hemisphere off limits. President Bonaparte refused to permit U.S. ships to send goods to either side, and would only permit trade if the foreign nation shipped the goods in their own ships. Since Britain and Germany dominated the Atlantic Ocean, they were able to strangle the French and Russians economically. The war came to an end after fifteen months of fighting and the Allies, led by Britain and Germany were victorious in 1914. Britain found herself in debt to the United States.

In 1843, Napoleon Bonaparte dies at the age of seventy-four. His body is entombed in a great monument in Washington City. Hundreds of thousands of people arrive from all over the United States to pay their respects to his passing. When Napoleon died, he left behind eight children; Napoleon, Carlo, Joseph, Letizia, Alexander, George Elisabeth, Matra and Andrew, and thirty-two grand-children. His life transformed the United States and the nature of the American people. He put an end to slavery and racial strife, and set America on a course that would make it the number one superpower by the beginning of the Twenti-eth Century.

# AFTERTHOUGHT

I know many who read this "What If" story might think this is a bit far-fetch, but it is based on an event that might have actually happened. I am referring to the possibility that Napoleon's parents after fleeing Corsica settled in America via England.

In 1768 the island of Corsica was ruled by the Italian city-state of Genoa. For sixty years the Corsicans fought Genoese rule. The leader of the rebels was Paoli. His trusted lieutenant was Carlo Buonaparte. (The name was later changed to Bonaparte by Napoleon).

On May 15, 1768, Louis XV, King of France bought the island from Genoa. In August, the French sent 10,000 troops and another 22,000 troops in March 1769. At first the Corsican rebels resisted French rule, but the French offered amnesty to anyone who agreed to accept French rule. Paoli decided to go into exile in England with over three hundred other rebels. Carlo, and his wife, Letizia thought seriously about joining their good friend, Paoli in exile. But they eventu-ally decided to remain in Corsica.

But what if Carlo and Letizia, who was pregnant with Napoleon, had decided to go to England in March 1769? Would they have remained in England, or resettle in England's North American colonies? Considering the anti-Catholic nature of English society, there is a good chance they would have resettled in America. Therefore, the possibility of Napoleon having been born in America four months after his parents left Corsica, was very real.

In my scenario Napoleon became good friends with Andrew Jackson. Jackson was a Jeffersonian Republican, and my Napoleon is a Hamiltonian Federalist, but in my story Jackson is won over by Napoleon. I based this on Jackson's actual opinion of Napoleon Bonaparte. He was a big admirer of Napoleon. In fact, Jackson was always something of a strange Jeffersonian. Jeffersonianism never fit him. That is why Jackson's brand of politics is referred to a Jacksonian Democracy. He combined the populism of Jefferson with own brand of militarism and authoritarianism. Let me quote from a book on Jackson by Michael Paul Rogin (page 73), "Fathers and Children."

"Jackson's hero in European politics was Napoleon, who had risen from obscurity to govern an empire. He admired the emperor's energy; his library contained five books on Napoleon. Should Napoleon invade England, he wrote in 1798, 'Tyranny will be humbled, throne crushed, and a republic will spring from the wreck, and millions of distressed people restored to the rights of man by the conquering arm of Bonaparte'...he (Jackson) invariably indicated sympathy with Caesar. It was a special sort of republican who chose Napoleon and Caesar for models."

Much of Napoleon's attitudes about the Indians and slaves reflect those that were the norms for America at the time. Since Napoleon and Jackson are good friends in my tale, I made Napoleon's feelings on race to mirror Jackson's. As for the colonization of all freed blacks to Liberia—that was almost an actual event. The American Colonization Society was actually founded in Washington and one of its supporters was James Monroe. It was responsible for the creation of the African nation of Liberia. It failed in its goal of colonizing all blacks in Liberia because the South refused to abandon slavery, and nothing short of a civil war could have made the South comply. The only way the society could have succeeded is if a Caesar-like leader supported it.

I also have Napoleon live longer than he does in reality. There has been much speculation about the cause of Napoleon's death. Some have claimed that he suffered from stomach cancer. I disagree. It is true he suffer from stomach pain, but never displayed symptoms associated with cancer. It is more likely he suffer from a stomach ulcer. Considering the life he led and the responsibilities and stress that was involved in his career, it is more likely a ulcer than cancer that he suffered from.

And there is also the belief that he was actually slowly poisoned by the British. Hair taken from Napoleon on his death bed has been analyzed and showed traces of arsenic. I am of the school that the British poisoned Napoleon. Despite all the glossing over of British behavior through the centuries, the British were ruthless. They did not forge the world's largest empire in the history of humanity by employing the Salvation Army, but through the most brutal application of the principles of Machiavelli and realpolitik.

In my alternate reality Napoleon did not have the formal education of a military academe, but instead learned the art of warfare on the battlefields of the American Revolution. In actually, Napoleon only had eighteen months of formal training in a military academe. He did possess an exceptional intellect that was the source of his greatness. Napoleon was unlike most generals who learned by experience on the battlefield a little at a time, throughout their long careers. He was a rare exception. He was the type of man who learned everything he knew about war from books at a very early age in his career. He once said, "He had fought over sixty battles, and did not know anything now that he did not know at the beginning." He was very cleaver at ripping out the guts of books, absorbing the ideas that belonged to other men, and possessed the unique powers to put into those ideas practice. This is a very rare ability. Combine this rare talent with the fact that he was not confronted with the combined armies of all the great powers of Europe, he is able to go on and achieve the permanent success that eluded the historical Napoleon. That is why the Napoleon in my reality is able to go on and achieve such great successes.

# WHAT IF THE ALLIES WON WORLD WAR ONE IN 1916?

## BY
## ROBERT BLUMETTI

In 1915 Winston Churchill, First Lord of the Admiralty, supported a plan for the invasion of the Dardanelles, calling for the capture of Gallipoli and then the capture the city of Constantinople. This would have resulted in the Turkish Empire being surrounded by Allied forces in 1915, thus forcing Turkey's withdrawal from the war. This would have prevented Bulgaria from joining into an alliance with Germany, and the Allies then could have supplied the Russian army by sending badly needed aid through the Black Sea. The Allies also would have been able to supply Serbia, which needed assistance to prevent the Central Powers from successfully overrunning the country.

The reason why this did not happen was the failure of the poorly planned Gallipoli Operation. The British Navy prematurely bombarded the Narrows and forced its way through the Dardanelles. Then, the British and French high commands delayed sending enough troops for the operation. A failure of will and poor planning by the Allies, who were not entirely behind the operation, believing their forces should be concentrated on the Western Front, permitted the Turks and Germans to build a new army strong enough to defend the Straits, in the next five weeks. But what would have happened if the British Navy had coordinated its attack with the British Army and the British and French provided the necessary resources from the very beginning?

# THE INVASION OF THE DARDANELLES

March 1915. General Sir Ian Hamilton convinced the British Navy to postpone the naval assault on the Dardanelles, and force the Narrows on March 15. He argued that it would give away their plans to land an invasion party in April. The Navy agreed. As a result, The Turks and Germans never suspected that the assault would come at the Dardanelles until it was too late. In Our Time Line the Germans and Turks realized that the Allies would follow up their naval assault with an invasion of the Gallipoli peninsula. They had five weeks to build a new army of 84,000 troops in place and waiting for the Allied assault. This does not happen.

April 1915. When the Allies finally assault the peninsula in April there are only 26,000 Turkish troops defending Gallipoli. The British and French high commands are committed to the invasion and provide the necessary troops in order to invade. One hundred and five thousand English, French, Australian and New Zealanders stormed onto the Gallipoli peninsula on April 25. There 26,000 Turkish troops are overwhelmed. The Naval assault, which includes ten British and five French battleships and begins to bombard the Turkish defenders from the rear. The landing party then make its way up the hill mass of Achi Baba. The ANZACS moved north of the promontory Gaba Tepe, driving the Turks from it and swinging inland, taking Hill 971. After Hill 971 was secured, the combined forces moved on Gallipoli.

The Germans and Turks rushed reserves to Gallipoli, but additional landings by the British from Saros Gulf, cut off the reserves from the mainland. On June 16, Gallipoli fell to the Allies. Allied ships were able to storm the Narrows and moved on to Constantinople. By August 1915, 600,000 British, French and ANZAC troops were thrown into the battle, and were soon in full control of the Dardanelles. Allied ships now flooded into the Sea of Marmara, while the Russian Black Sea Fleet laid siege to the Bosporus from the East. Constantinople was cut off. All of European Turkey was occupied by Allied troops with the exception of Constantinople. Allied forces landing in July and August occupied Chanak on the Asian side of the Narrows. On September 9, Constantinople, was captured. Turkey. overwhelmed by the assault, dropped out of the war on September 11.

# BULGARIA, GREECE AND SERBIA

King Ferdinand of Bulgaria was related to the Kaiser. The Bulgarian Army had 300,000 troops and 600,000 reservists. The Bulgarians were of warrior stock were expert at fighting in rough terrain, but the Bulgarian Army lacked adequate artillery. The Germans and the Bulgarians had been talking about Bulgaria entering the war on the side of the Central Powers, but the King delayed giving the Germans an answer. He wanted to wait and see how the Allied invasion of the Dardanelles turned out. When the Turks surrendered, the King decided to enter the war on the side of the Allies.

The Serbs had been holding off the Austrians for a year. The Serbians, exhausted but determined not to surrender, were able to stop the Austrians from invading Serbia. After one year of fighting their army was reduced to 200,000 men.

Greece had offered to join the Allies after the Turks entered the war on the side of the Central Powers. The Greek Army number 240,000 and possessed strong artillery. The Greek Army was willing to attack Constantinople, but the Russians refused to support them because Russia had its own designs on the city. Greece did not enter the war because King Constantine was related to the Kaiser and was able to use the Russian refusal as an excuse to remain neutral. On September 21, Premier Venizelos of Greece asked the Allies for 150,000 troops. Greece and Bulgaria entered the war on the side of the Allies on October 2, 1915.

The Russians drove into Turkish Armenia in November 1915, under the command of General Nikolai Yudenich. He quickly captured the cities of Erzurum, Tribizond and Erzancan before the Turks surrendered. Thousands of Armenians were being killed by the Turks. The Russians were welcomed by the Christian Armenians as liberators from the Moslem butchers. General Yudenich became a hero to the Armenians.

General Sir Archibald Murry occupied Palestine and Syria, while General Charles Townsend occupied Baghdad, while the Italians land in southern Asia Minor.

# THE PROGRESSION OF THE WAR DURING 1915 ON OTHER FRONTS

Under General Mackensen, the Germans were forming an army of 200,000 to attack Serbia in 1915. They were planning on Bulgaria entering the war on their side, but Bulgaria joined the Allies instead. Mackensen called off the offensive and ordered his troops to construct a defensive line in Bosnia.

Two hundred thousand British and French troops poured into Greece and moved north into Serbia. They were joined by 100,000 Bulgarian troops and another 100,000 Greek troops. By March 1916 there were over 600,000 troops in Serbia.

During 1915 the Western Front remained stabile, but the Russians were forced to retreat all along the Eastern Front. From May 2 to September 30, the Austro-German armies forced the Russians back, from of Poland and Lithuania to a line running south of Riga on the Baltic Sea, east to Dvinsk, and south, just west of Minsk, through the Pripet Marshes to Galicia and the Rumanian border.

# THE EASTERN FRONT 1915

The Russians caved in after the Austro-German attack in Galicia. The Russian Third Army was virtually destroyed. By May, the Germans reached the San River. In June a war council was held by the High Command of Germany at Pless. The Kaiser, General Conrad of Austria, Falkenhayn, Ludendorff, Hindenburg, Hoffman and Mackensen were all present. There was plenty for them to talk about. Italy had joined the war on the side of the Allies. The Allies were ashore in Gallipoli. Conrad wanted to transfer divisions from Galicia to the Italian Front. All the Germans disagreed. They wanted to continue the offensive against Russia, but Falkenhayn was becoming anxious about the Dardanelles. But he knew there was little that could be done to hold Turkey. He urged four divisions be transferred to France. He hoped this would cause the Allies to cease sending additional troops to Turkey.

The Kaiser decided to ignore Turkey and continue the offensive against Russia. Hindenburg and Ludendorff hoped to deliver a knock out blow to Russia before the end of the year. Then the Germans could divert troops to the Balkans in an attack on Serbia in the Fall.

The Germans and the Austrians continued to push the Russians back, through Poland to Riga and Minsk. But try as they might, they could not deliver their longed-for knock out push. The Russians were able to withdraw most of their armies in tact, though they lost 500,000 prisons to the Germans in doing so. The German offensive came to a halt in September. They gained much ground but failed to achieve their main objective, crushing the Russian armies.

The Grand Duke resigned as commander of the Russian armies and the Czar placed himself in his place. On September 5, Czar Nicholas II signed the order reading: "Today I have taken supreme command of all forces of the sea and land armies operating in the theater of war. We will fulfill our sacred duty to defend our country to the last. We will not dishonor the Russian land."

The Russian soldier fought with bravery, but the Germans prevailed because of vastly superior firepower. The Germans outgunned the Russians in machine guns by 4 to 1. Russian artillery was vastly inferior to German artillery. The Russians lacked enough rifles for all their soldiers and even less cartridges. Unarmed men waited in line for their comrades to be shot so they might inherit their rifles. Yet there was no route, no panic and no mutiny. The Russian armies retreated in good order.

The Czar was determined to tough it out. He was adamantly against a separate peace with the Germans. He was hoping the Allies could knock Turkey out of the war. With the Straits in Allied hands, Britain and France could supply Russia with the necessary arms to stop the Germans and go on the offensive. General Mikail Alekseev manned the front during the winter months of 1915-16. He did an excellent job of maintaining the front and preventing it from collapsing. During the winter, the Russian Duma in St. Petersburg issued charges of treason. Claiming that the Russian banks and many Russian industrialists were in league with the Germans. This led to a rise in public anxiety. Pavel Milyukov representing the Left within the Duma, called for the Duma to take control of the war effort. Nicholas disbanded the Duma on advice of Premier Ivan Goremykun. This results in riots in many cities. With rioting getting out of control, Nicholas if forced to restore the Duma. The crisis so passed. Nicholas swore he will have his revenge on the Duma.

In January 1916, the Germans are forced to transfer 400,000 troops from the Eastern Front to the Balkans to meet the growing number of Allied troops organizing in Serbia during the winter of 1915-16.

Falkenhayn wanted to conduct an attack in the West against Verdun, but because of the Allied build-up in Serbia and the entry of Bulgaria and Greece into the war, he was forced to call off his plans. The Germans had to remain on the defensive in the West. It was even agreed that the German Army should begin constructing a stronger defensive line one hundred miles to the rear of the front. When it was completed, the German Army would withdraw to this stronger position so as to be in a better position to defend itself against a possible Allied attack in 1916.

# THE DEATH OF LORD KITCHENER

Lord Kitchener was the most famous soldier in the British Empire. He was Prime Minister and head of the War Ministry. He had also developed a warm and close relationship with Czar Nicholas II of Russia. With the collapse of Turkey and supplies flooding into Russia, Kitchener decided to pay the Czar a visit to coordinate a joint attack on Germany and Austria in 1916. Kitchener boarded the cruiser, the Hampshire. As it left Britain, it struck a mine in the North Sea and sunk in five minutes. All but twelve people disappeared into the icy cold waters of the North Sea, including Lord Kitchener. The sea claimed the great man. His replacement was Lloyd George. Lloyd George was disliked by King George V of England and his dislike was conveyed to his cousin, the Czar. Kitchener's death and his replacement of Lloyd George caused a chill between Russia and Britain.

# THE RUSSIAN OFFENSIVE OF 1916

With Western supplies flooding into Russia through the Black Sea, the Russian army were now well equipped. Gone were days of shortages of supplies, lack the of rifles and ammunition. The Russians planned a major offensive for June, 1916. General Aleksei Brusilov decided to attack the Austro-German forces at their weakest point in Galicia. He realized the Germans were forced to transfer many of their finest troops to the Balkans. He also knew that the Austrian armies were filled with disgruntled Slavs, Italians, and Romanians who hated the Habsburg Empire. Another reason for selecting Galicia was its closeness to Romania, which though neutral, was talking about entering the war against the Central Powers. By June, the Russian armies now had enough machine guns and artillery to launch their offensive.

In June 1916, the Russian South West Army group attacked. It crushed through the Austrian defenses along a two hundred mile front and rushed westward to the Carpathian Mountains. The Austrian Fourth and Seventh armies reeled and collapsed under the onslaught. The Russians got to the Carpathian passes in late June. The Austrians fought well, but by mid-July, the Russians captured the passes. It would prove to be a mortal blow for the dual monarchy.

Hindenburg rushed every available German division he could spare from the already overstretched Western Front to Hungary. Yet, it wasn't enough. Brusilov resumed the offensive with fresh supplies and reinforcements in August. He kept advancing into September. His fame became worldwide, for he was winning the war in the east. The Teutonic armies had thus far lost 600,000 Germans and another 400,000 Austrians (mostly Slavs and Romanians) fell into captivity. The Russians lost an equal number, but because their vast manpower and endless supplies from the Western Allies, the Russians were better able to sustain more loses.

# THE BALKAN OFFENSIVE OF 1916

The Allies in Serbia now launched a major attack in July 1916. After three weeks of heavy fighting in the mountains of Bosnia, the Austrians were overpowered and soon were fleeing west. In the second week of August, the Allies stormed across the Danube River at Belgrade, into Hungary. On August 27, Romania declared war on Austria-Hungary. Three Romanian armies invaded Transylvania. The Russians now broke out of the Carpathian Mountains and flooded into the Hungarian plains. Austrian defenses crumbled. Allied armies were now marching on Budapest, the capital of Hungary from the north, east and south.

# THE WESTERN FRONT 1916

The Western front remained remarkably stabled during 1915 and into 1916. Germany's plans for an offensive were canceled. Divisions had to be transferred to other fronts. The Germans concentrated on constructing a new defensive line to their rear. The British were planning a big push. General Haig was planning an offensive at the Somme River. The French General Joffie agreed to coordinate a French attack between Soissons and Reims, creating a double pincer movement where the Germans were at their weakest. The attack on the Somme began on July 15. Over 60,000 British troops were killed in the first assault. The French attack took place three days later, fairing no better. But the German line was becoming dangerously thin. The Allies kept up their attacks despite their loses. In August, Haig was ready to unleash his new weapon. For weeks he was stockpiling the first tanks.

The Germans were slowly withdrawing their forces to the new line they had constructed. It ran from Cambrai in the north. Through St. Quentin to Laon in the south Haig used the first forty-two tanks to support an attack by twelve divisions on September 15. The rumbling monsters scared the Germans out of their wits. The German High Command was unable to react in time. The tanks ripped open a small hole in the German line between Cambrai and St. Quentin. Haig, sensing the opportunity, poured through with his reserves. Due more to desperation than insight, Haig sought to match the Russian successes on the Eastern

Front and the gamble paid off. The British and French armies were able to break through the new German defensive line and push the German armies back even further. The Germans, after regaining their composure, withdrew in an orderly fashion. The shock of the first tanks wore off and the Germans were able to form a new front running from Zee Brigge on the North Sea coast, south to the French frontier east of Lide. From Lide it ran along the Franco-Belgian border to Mezieres, and then south to Verdun. The Germans were able to reestablish the front and halt the Allied advance in November 1916.

# THE COLLAPSE OF CENTRAL POWERS.

During the summer of 1916, Emperor Joseph of Austria died at the age of 86. His successor was his grandnephew, Charles Francis Joseph. Charles's new Foreign Minister was Count Ottokar Czernin who wanted an armistice. He could see the Habsburg Empire collapsing all around him and hoped to preserve the monarchy by making a separate peace with the Allies. General Conrad resigned his post in October 1916. With the Russian armies moving on Bratislava, the Russians now threatened to occupy all of Moravia and Bohemia. The Czechs rebelled in Prague and the Croatians and Slovenians welcomed the Allies as liberators. Budapest is occupied by the British, French, Serbs and Russians on November 1. On November 5, the Austrians asked for an armistice with the Allies. Austria-Hungary officially surrenders three days later.

In Poland, the Russians continued their offensive against the Germans. With the collapse of the Austrians, Brusilov was able to concentrate his attack on the Germans, with the Germans inflicting great causalities on the Russians. With the collapse of the Austrians, the Germans decided that the war was lost. The High Command tells the Kaiser to contact his cousin Czar Nicholas of Russia and request a meeting.

In Russia, the "Mad Monk" Rasputin had won favor with the Czarina and the Czar by claiming he could heal their son Alexis, who suffered from hemophilia. Two ambitious men, Alexander Protopopv, who became Minister of the Interior, and Boris Stuermer became Foreign Minster, feared revolution and feared that if the German monarchy collapsed, the Romanov monarchy may soon follow. They worked out a deal with the Germans. They convinced the Czar to meet with the Kaiser in person. On November 9, the two emperors met in the city of Dvinsk on the Eastern front. They discussed terms for an armistice. A cease fire was called later that day and Germany formally surrendered on November 11, 1916.

# KAISER-CZAR MEETING

The British and French protested the meeting between the Kaiser and the Czar, but Nicholas agreed to meet with his cousin the Russians were exhausted. Sensing the Germans' situation was becoming especially desperate, the Czar decided to present terms to the Kaiser that were generous. The Czar was concerned about the rising discontent within Germany and a possible Marxist-socialist revolution if Germany was harshly punished. The Czar was concerned about preserving the integrity of Absolute Monarchism, both aboard and within Russia.

Since the Germans still occupied Lithuania and most of Poland, the Czar first demanded the Germans withdraw from all former Russian territories. The Kaiser agreed. The Czar demanded only the German province of Posen, which was mostly Polish in population. The Kaiser also agreed to the annexation of Galicia from Austria. In return, the Czar agreed to the preservation of the German monarchy.

In Austria, revolution broke out in Vienna. Emperor Charles was forced to flee to Germany. He pleaded with the Kaiser and the Czar to restore his monarchy, but the Kaiser couldn't and the Czar refused, fearing he would alienate the different Slavic nationalist groups demanding independence in the former Habsburg empire. The Kaiser and the Czar decided that a plebiscite should be held in the former Austrian territories of Burgenland, Bohemia and Moravia. Some pan-Slavic minister within the Russian government wanted to create a Greater Czech state, but the Czar felt that would jeopardize the right of Absolute Monarchism. The Czechs wanted a republic, and Czech leaders were republicans. The Czar feared a Czech state would spread republicanism throughout Eastern Europe and the Balkans. A strong, but subservient German monarchy was more to Russia's liking, for it would increase the power of monarchism in Europe. The needs of the Romanov monarchy out weighed the demands of pan-Slavism.

The Anglo-Franco-Italian Allies agreed to accept the Russo-German agreement, but there was a great deal of bad feelings in the West toward the Czar and the Russians. When the Russo-German armistice was announced on November 11, 1916, the Germans still occupied most of Belgium, and some French territory. Russia to permitted the German army to remain in place until a peace treaty was signed. The French protested and wanted all territories evacuated by the Germans, but the Czar refused. The Czar hoped that by keeping the Germans in place, the French would be forced to support a quick conclusion to the negotiations and the signing of a peace treaty.

President Wilson won reelection in November, 1916 by promising to keep America out of the war in Europe. The first thing he did was offer to mediate among the warring powers. Both the Allies and the Germans refused Wilson's offer (Britain was not as deeply in debt to the United States as she was in our time line because the war ended two years earlier).

A conference was held in Vienna on January 12, 1917. After just seven days, the parties at the conference signed a peace treaty. The Germans had already withdrawn from Russian territories in the east back in November, while their armies remained in place in the west until after the treaty was signed. This caused the Western Powers to become suspicious of Russia motives toward Germany. The news media in Britain and France began making charges of a Russo-German conspiracy. There were charges that the Czar was another Ivan the Terrible, and Jewish interest groups in Britain, France and even in the United States made claims of another anti-Jewish pogrom being conducted by the Czarist secret police.

# THE TREATY OF VIENNA

The treaty of Vienna was compared to the Congress of Vienna held in 1815 after the defeat of Napoleon. All parties were involved, including the defeated power. The treaties were negotiated and not dictated by the victors as the Treaty of Versailles was in our time line. There was also a division between the Russians and Prussians on one side and the French and the British on the other.

Germany was not forced to pay indemnities to the victors, but agreed to make interest-free loans to Russia, France and Belgium to rebuild their territories. It was agreed that the loans were to be repaid, but everyone understood that they would never be repaid. This arrangement gave the appearance of sound economic transactions that prevented an economic crisis in Germany or anywhere else in Europe.

The Western Allies agreed to a plebiscite in Austrian territories. The Italians protested, demanding all of South Tyrol. Eventually they acquiesced when the Russians hinted that they would try to prevent the Italians from annexing Dalmatia if they didn't agree to the plebiscite. The Russians then demanded a greater South Slavic state led by the Serbs. The Kingdom of the Yugoslavs was created. When Italy demanded Dalmatia, the Serbs protested. Britain and France supported Italy. The Russians protested, but they had already agreed Italy should get Dalmatia. In this way, the Russians presented themselves as a friend of their brother Slavs and won the support the Serbs to the Russian camp.

Turkey was completely partitioned according to a secret Allied treaty. Bulgaria received all of European Turkey with the exception of Gallipoli and Constantinople, which were given to Russia. Russia also annexed the Asia shore of the Straits. Greece annexed the Aegean shore of Asia Minor, and Italy annexed the southern half of Asia Minor. The French annexed greater Syria. The Russians annexed Turkish Armenia and the British annexed all of Mesopotamia, the Persian Gulf, Palestine and Jordan.

The French wanted revenge against Germany for their defeat in the Franco-Prussian War of 1870. They wanted to annex Alsace-Lorraine, the Saarland, and create a separate Rhineland Republic under French control. The Russians and Germans refused. When Germany agreed to surrender all her oversea colonies, the British agreed and supported the Russians. The only territory the Germans lost in the west was Alsace-Lorraine, which was annexed by France. The German Cameroons were given to France. German East Africa and South West Africa was annexed by the British Empire. Togoland was partition by the French and the British. Italy did not receive any former German colonies in Africa. Instead, Britain turned over a small part of Kenya to Italy, and the French surrendered some desert lands to the Italians in Libya. The Italians demanded they be permitted to annex Ethiopia as compensation, but France and Britain refused their demands. German territories in China were given to Japan and all her islands were divided between Japan and Britain.

A plebiscite was eventually held on March 1, 1917 in the former Austrian territories. All the Austrian territories, Burgenland, the northern half of South Tyrol, Carniola and the German inhabited Sudetenland voted to become part of Germany. The Czech inhabited areas of Bohemia and Moravia were united in the independent Grand Duchy of Bohemia. Hungary became a shrunken kingdom. Transylvania was annexed by Romania.

In Asia, Russia annexed northern Persia and the British annexed the southeastern part of the country. The remainder of Persia became an independent Persian state. Russia also annexed Sinkiang and Mongolia from China, as well as northern Manchuria, while Japan annexed southern Manchuria, and the British annexed Tibet. The rest of China remained independent, but occupied by the British, French and the Japanese. These three powers signed a secret proposal to eventually partition and annex the rest of China at some future date.

# THE RUSSIAN EMPIRE

With the victory of 1916 and the Treaty of Vienna, the Czar's popularity soared. He was hailed as the greatest Russian Czar since Peter the Great. The power and popularity of the Romanov dynasty under Nicholas II was never greater. Some of the Czar's advisers pressured the Czar to disband the Duma. One of these advisers was the "Mad Monk", Rasputin. The Czar agreed and disbanded the Duma, declaring the sovereignty of the Absolute Monarchy in the Russian Empire. This caused some radical socialists and anarchists to turn to political violence. Rumor spread that Rasputin was behind the Czar's decision to disband the Duma. A group of radical anarchists decided to assassinate him.

Rasputin warned the Czar in 1915 that he would be assassinated. The only question was by whom? He said that if he was killed by aristocrats, it would result in the destruction of the Romanov monarchy in Russia. But if he was killed by the masses, the monarchy would survive. On May 23, Rasputin was captured and his body was chopped into many small pieces and set on fire. His horrible death engaged the Czar, but Rasputin's prophecy came true. In 1917 the Russian Empire stretched from the Danube to the Pacific Ocean. A stronger and larger Germany was allied to Russia. Russian troops occupied Hungary, and the shrunken state of Turkey. Romania, Bohemia, Bulgaria, Yugoslavia, and Greece were pro-Russian. Constantinople and the Straits were annexed by Russia, as well as part of Persia and half of China. The Russian Empire had never been larger or stronger.

In the West, especially in Britain, France and the United States, liberals began to wail about the growing threat of "Czarism" to democracy. Jewish groups also began calling for a crusade against "Czarism." Because of the restrictive nature of Russian policy toward Jews within Russia, Jewish groups have been conducting an anti-Russian campaign for twenty years. But in the years after the Great War their warnings became shrill. In 1917, Jewish financier Jacob Schiff agreed to financed Leon Trotsky and one hundred other communists with twenty million dollars, sending them to Russia to work for a Marxist revolution in Russia. Trotsky and his fellow communists secretly arrived in Helsinki through Sweden. He began organizing red cells in Petrograd. But the Russian secret police caught wind of Trotsky's activities. Trotsky was planning on a series of riots in several major Russian cities which he hoped would ignite a revolution. But in June 1918, he was arrested and executed. Most of the communist agents who arrived with him were either arrested or fled. Czar Nicholas proclaimed a victory over communism in Russia. In Switzerland, Lenin followed closely the events unfolding in Russia. He told his fellow Reds in Switzerland that Trotsky's failure had doomed Marxism in Russia. Lenin became so depressed that within a year he suffered a stroke. He would die on November 1, 1919.

# FRENCH SUPPORT FOR POPULAR NATIONALISM IN ITALY AND GERMANY

During the war the French government was supporting nationalist groups in Italy. The French paid large sums of money for people like Benito Mussolini to advocate Italy's entering the war on the side of the Allies. After the war, Mussolini was still receiving money from the French to advocate that Italy join the anti-Russian alliance with France, Britain and Japan. The Italian monarchy resisted the idea of an anti-Russian alliance. Mussolini formed a group he called the Fascist Nationalist Party and began attacking both communists and monarchists. In 1922 he led a "March on Rome." The Italian Monarchy was forced to flee and Mussolini set up the Italian Fascist Republic. The first thing he did was announce that Italy would join the anti-Russian alliance.

In Germany, the Social Democratic Party had splintered after the war. The majority socialist remained within the Social Democratic Party, while the minority socialist formed the German Communist Party. Red revolts erupted in Saxony, Bavaria and in the Ruhr, but they were all unsuccessful. The German army remained loyal to the Kaiser and quickly put down all rebellions. (In our time line the communist set up a soviet republic in Bavaria. Most of the leaders were Jewish. Most of the leaders of the Communist movement under Lenin, in Russia, were also Jewish. This helped to contribute to the rise of and extreme form of anti-Semitism in Germany. Since there were no successful Marxist revolutions, the German right never developed this extreme anti-Semitism. The Communist Party was disbanded in Germany and the government was dominated by the German Nationalist Party (DNP) and the Nationalist People's Party of Germany (NVPD). Both these parties supported the monarchy, but there rose up radical nationalist-volkish groups that opposed the pro-Russian alliance. They hated the Slavs and supported a program of eastern expansion. (In this time line the French never separated the Saarland from Germany, or occupied the Rhineland and the Ruhr. Anti-French sentiment was not as strong in Germany).

As in Italy, the French hoped to support nationalist groups who opposed the new German-Russian alliance. One small party the French began channeling money to was the German People's Party based in Munich. It was founded by Anton Drexler, Karl Harrer and Dietrich Eckart in 1917. In 1918, a newly released veteran by the name of Adolf Hitler joined the German People's Party. He soon proved himself to be an excellent organizer and orator. In 1919 he changed the name of the party to the National Socialist German People's Party (NSDVP) and quickly became its leader. He too accepted money from the French, and advocated an end to the German-Russian alliance.

# THE BRITISH FEDERATION OF NATIONS

The British and French refused to repay their bills to the United States. Because the Great War lasted only two years, the Allies did not go as deep into debt that they did in our time line. The British did not have to sell off as much of their financial resources to pay for the war as they did in our time line. The British economy came through the war in much better shape. Britain retained the status as the strongest nation in the world, though it was slightly weaker than it was in 1914, though the United States had a stronger economy. But the United States remained isolationist. A reaction to Allied refusal to repay their war debts, soared American interest in participating in world events.

The world economy was split. The German-Russian block controlled the vast resources of half of Europe, all of Russia and half of Asia. The Russian army was the largest in the world. The German army was rapidly rebuilding itself. German financiers were invited to invest in Russia and central Europe. In ten years, the Germans dominated the vast Russo-German space that stretched from the Rhine to the Pacific. There were now two economies; the Russo-German landmass, and the rest of the world.

The economies after the war quickly recovered. All nations relied on John Maynard Keynes' economic theory of deficit spending by the government. Because Winston Churchill was renown as the military genius behind the invasion of Gallipoli, which resulted in the defeat of the Central Powers, he became Prime Minister of Britain in 1917. Churchill worked hard to maintain British supremacy throughout the world. He was the architect who constructed the anti-Russian alliance. He renewed the Anglo-Japanese Alliance in 1922, and worked to establish an alliance with Italy. After Mussolini came to power in Italy, Churchill paid him a state visit and signed the Anglo-Franco-Italian naval treaty to jointly police the Mediterranean Sea. Beginning in 1900, it was the custom of the British to invite the Premiers of Canada, Australia, South Africa and New Zealand to visit London and discuss common interests. Churchill always supported Cecil Rhodes' dream of establishing a British World Federation that included the United States. Churchill was disappointed by American refusal to move closer to England. He worked to set up the foundation of Rhodes' federation. In 1924, the Treaty of British Federation was signed. England, Scotland, Northern Ireland, Wales, Australia, New Zealand, Canada, and South Africa all signed the treaty. Each state was an equal partner in the British Federation of Nations and all sent delegates to the Federal Parliament. Churchill was no longer the Prime Minister of Great Britain, but of the British Federation of Nations. Each member had a premier who governed over domestic policies. The white states of the British Empire were now united as one nation. Plans were being made to admit the white settled areas of Southern Rhodesia and Kenya highlands in the near future.

When riots broke out in India, Churchill moved rapidly. Mohandas Gandhi was leading an independence movement. Though he advocated peaceful protest, riots soon broke out. Churchill was determined not to lose the most precious jewel in the British crown. He sent in additional troops and fired on the rioters. The troops opened fire and killed thousands. Gandhi was arrested and executed him for treason in 1926. There was a public outcry by the Labor Party at Churchill's ruthlessness, and he was referred to as the British Czar. Churchill survived as Prime Minister for several more months, but he had to resign in January, 1927, three months after the world was plunged into the Great Depression.

# THE GREAT DEPRESSION OF 1926

After ten years of ever extending themselves, the financial houses of the world were forced to retract their investments. Loans were called in and the Stock Markets of the world began falling after several banks failed, setting off a domino effect that stretched around the world. All the major industrial countries were badly affected by the economic crash. Unemployment rose sharply. Businesses closed and banks collapsed. The United States and Germany, the two most industrialized countries, were the most affected by the depression. In Russia economic disruption had a terrible affect in the cities. Most farmers refused to send their goods to market in the cities. Foot riots broke out in most major cities.

# THE UNITED STATES ELECTIONS

In 1920 the Republicans recaptured the White House. The Socialists were gaining strength in the United States throughout the last ten years, and labor radicalism was increasing. The "Red Scare" gripped America. The Democrats nominated James. Cox of Ohio and Franklin D. Roosevelt, of New York. The

Republicans nominated Governor Calvin Coolidge of Massachusetts, because he made an instant reputation in 1919 when he called out the National Guard to end a police strike in Boston and Charles G. Dawes of Illinois as his running mate. Coolidge won with 20 million votes against 5 million for Cox and 1.2 million for Eugene V. Debs, the Socialist candidate. Coolidge proved to be a conservative and strong president. He supported business, refused to tolerate socialist extremism, and gave the American people a sense of confidence in the country once more. In 1924 Coolidge reluctantly agreed to run for a second term. The Democrats were a divided party.

The Ku Klux Klan was reborn in 1915 in Georgia. By 1924 it was a powerful organization throughout the country, claiming five million members. The Klan was anti-Catholic, anti-Jewish, anti-black and anti-immigrant. By 1924 they were a power to be reckoned with in the Democratic Party. The most popular candidate in the Democratic Party was New York Governor Al Smith. The Klan opposed him because he was Catholic. The Klan defeated Smith's attempt to get the nomination, but failed to nominate its candidate, William G. McAdoo of California. A compromise candidate John W. Davis was chosen. In 1924 Coolidge won reelection with 21 million votes, Davis actually came in third with three million votes behind the leftist Progressive Party candidate, Robert M. La Follette, who received five million votes.

When the Great Depression arrived, Coolidge was very popular, but his popularity quickly declined. The Democrats and the Progressives both blamed the depression on him, and accused the Republicans of being cronies of capitalist robber barons. In 1928 Hebert Hoover was the Republican candidate Al Smith, was able to win the Democratic nomination because the Klan lost much of its power in 1926 due to several scandals among their leadership. This time, the socialists and progressives decided to support Smith. Both Smith and Hoover received 18 million votes, but Smith received a majority of the electoral college votes and won.

# THE RISE OF NATIONAL SOCIALISM IN GERMANY

With the onset of the Great Depression, the little known National Socialist German People's Party (NSDVP) became the second largest party in Germany in the 1927 elections. The German National Party (DNP) remained the largest but lost half of its seats in the Reichstag. The Social Democrats (SDP) and the Center Party (CP) were next, and last was the German Nationalist People's Party

(DNVP). Hitler immediately became a national figure. Political unrest and economic hardship spread throughout Germany. Extremist socialist groups broke away from the SDP and conducted a terrorist campaign. The Storm Troopers of the NSDVP conducted a campaign of warfare against leftist groups and pro-monarchy groups. In another election that was called in 1930, the NSDVP became the largest party in Germany. Chancellor Bruening wanted to declare marshal law and disband the Reichstag. The Kaiser refused. He feared civil war. The German army agreed that the threat of civil war was too great. A second election was held in 1930 and this time the NSDVP received 51% of the vote. Kaiser William II suffered a stroke and dies in October 1930. His son is crown William III. He calls Adolf Hitler to Berlin and appoints him Chancellor.

The first thing Hitler does, is declare marshal law and outlaws all political parties except the NSDVP, DNVP and the DNP. Ernst Rhoem, the leader of his Strom Troopers, was advocating a second revolution. He wanted to confiscate all estates of the Junker Class and replace the army with the Storm Troopers. The Army was concerned and feared a civil war. There were four million members in the Storm Troopers, and the army had five hundred thousand soldiers. Many of its reserves were actually members of the Storm Troopers and could not be depended upon. The generals, led by Ludendorff, even feared that many of their soldiers were secretly members of Hitler's party and would rebel. Hitler let Rhoem threaten the ruling classes of Germany while he secretly met with the leaders of the German army. Hitler met with Ludendorff and promised to stop the Storm Troopers, arrest Rhoem, and defend the army, in exchange for the army's agreement to force William III to abdicate, suspend the monarchy, a thus make Hitler dictator of Germany with the title of Fuehrer. Ludendorff remembered how he was a virtual dictator of Germany during the Great War, and wanted that power again. He hoped to make Hitler the ruler of Germany, but intended to control Hitler and rule through him. But Hitler was able to isolate Ludendorff and eventually forced him into retirement.

On June 3, William the III abdicated and Hitler was declared dictator of Germany with the support of the army. On June 15, 1931, Hitler arrested Rhoem and the leadership of the Storm Troopers. Within three months, Hitler announced that all parties except the NSDVP were outlawed in Germany. Thus, the Third Reich was born. Hitler begins to transform Germany society. Through a program of public works and the modernization of the army and air force, Hitler is able to eliminate unemployment and revitalize the Germany economy. The Nuremberg Laws are passed that instituted a set of racial policies denying rights to Jews and Slavs. Former Prime Minister Churchill pays Hitler a visit and praises the German Fuehrer for rebuilding Germany. Hitler renounces all claims to Alsace-Lorraine and signs a friendship treaty with France. Mussolini is invited to Germany and the two dictators declare their opposition to Absolute Monarchism. Jews are encouraged to migrate.

# ECONOMIC AND POLITICAL UNREST IN THE RUSSIAN EMPIRE

Czar Nicholas II had the laws changed to permit a woman to become Czar once more. He knew that his son would never live long enough to rule. In 1922 the law was finally change. In 1923 Czarevich Alexis died. Nicholas appoints his eldest daughter, Olga, as his heir. The depression hit Russia hard. The Russians have been spending a great deal of their resources to maintain control of their vast Eurasian empire. Millions are unemployed and there isn't enough food reaching the major cities. Demonstrations spread throughout the empire. Non-Russian nationalities are especially rebellious. The Russian government spreads propaganda blaming the Jews for the crisis. Anti-Jewish riots break out and thousands are killed. Most of the Russian troops are withdrawn from the Balkans to deal with unrest at home. In time the government is able to suppress the rebellions and order is restored. Millions of people are sent into exile, and resettled in colonies in Siberia, Manchuria, central Asia and Mongolia. The Czarist government is even more authoritarian and most rights have been repealed. The stress of the unrest and repression necessary to restore order caused great physical toll on the Czar. In 1937 he suffers a heart attack and dies. His oldest daughter is crown Czarina Olga.

Tension rises in Europe between Russia and the new Germany. Hitler is rebuilding the German army and air force. In 1933 Hitler withdraws Germany from its alliance with Russia. In 1934 Hitler signs a mutual defense alliance with Italy, France, Britain and Japan. After Russian troops withdraw from Hungary, Yugoslavia, Romania and Bulgaria, Germany signs non-aggression pacts with Hungary and Romania.

In the Far East the Japanese and Russian armies suffer a series of clashes in Manchuria and Mongolia in May 1938. The clashes continue throughout the summer of 1938. Hitler takes advantage of Russian preoccupation with Japan to put pressure on Bohemia. Hitler claims the small German minority in Bohemia is being persecuted and threatens to invade Bohemia. The Russian generals demand that the Czarina declare war on Japan. The Japanese navy bombs Vladivostok in July. Russia declares war on Japan on August 1, 1938. On August 3, Germany occupies Bohemia. Russia declares war on Germany twenty-four hours later. By August 6, Britain, France and Italy have all declared war on Russia. The Second World War has begun.

# THE UNITED STATES DURING THE DEPRESSION

President Smith begins to push for reforms that will turn the economy around. He belongs to the progressive wing of the Democratic party. Smith's program is not every different from the one FDR would propose in OTL. He is faced with opposition from both within the Democratic Party, led by Randolph Hearst and a resurgent Klan, and from the Republicans. Every effort President Smith makes to reform the banks and push through public works programs are stopped by the Congress and the courts. Then, in 1927 Smith take the United States off the gold standard. This causes an outrage among Americans most well-place financiers and top industrialists.

A group is formed by some of the wealthiest men in America called the Liberty League. It is financed by such powerful corporations as J. P. Morgan, Du Pont, General Motors and U. S. Steel. Irene Du Pont, as supporter of racial eugenics and Fascism, as well as E. F. Hutton, Robert S. Clark, H. S. McKay and John Davis, former leader of the Democratic Party seek out General MacArthur and convinces him to lead a paramilitary force of veterans supported by the Liberty League. In the summer of 1928 MacArthur leads a march of hundreds of thousands of veterans on Washington, and demand the bonus that was promised to the veterans ten years earlier. The situation gets out of hand and soon violence breaks out. MacArthur leads his forces and storms the White House. President Smith is captured and forced to agree to marshal law. The Law for the restoration of the United States returns America to the gold standard, and transform the President into a figurehead. MacArthur was appointed Secretary of General Affairs, a post that replaces the Secretary of State, and is given dictatorial powers. The office of the Vice President is eliminated. The United States became a Fascist dictatorship controlled by the most powerful and wealthiest families in America.

# WORLD WAR TWO

German armies crash through Poland, smashing three Russian armies. Three hundred-thousand Russians are taken prisoner near Posen. Another Russian army is crushed as it tried to invade East Prussia. Four hundred-thousand additional Russians are captured near Warsaw. In two weeks the Germany overruns Poland and invades Lithuania. The Germans use a new tactic known as Blitzkrieg (lightning warfare). By the first week of September 1938, the German panzer armies are racing toward Riga and Minsk. By September 23, German forces surround and capture four hundred-thousand Russian troops near Minsk. Other German forces move through Galicia and enter the Ukraine. Romania and Hungary declare war on Russia on September 25. The Romanians invade Bessarabia. By October 1, German troops have occupied the Baltic states and Smolensk has fallen, and Kiev is under siege. Germany invades Finland in the north. The Finns rebel against the Russians. The Balts and Ukrainians welcome the Germans as liberators. By October 15, Petrograd is besieged and other five hundred-thousand Russian troops surrender in eastern Ukraine. Over three million Russian troops have surrendered.

Clashes break out in Asia Minor. Turkey declares war on Russia attacks the Dardanelles while the British, French and Italian fleets bombard the Straits. Russian and British troops clash in Persia and China. Japan now pours hundreds of thousands of troops into Manchuria and China. Yugoslavia and Bulgaria enters the war on Russia's side on September 10. Greece declares war on Russia after signing a treaty with Britain and Italy promising Constantinople to Greece. On September 30, Yugoslavia is invaded by Italy, Germany, Hungary, Romania and by the French and British through Greece. Romanian troops invade Bulgaria. On October 16, Constantinople surrenders to Allied armies. In the Far East the Japanese take Vladivostok and occupy northern Sakalin Island. On November 1, Czarina Olga announces that Russia surrenders.

# THE TREATY OF BERLIN

Czarina Olga signs the Treaty of Berlin on February 2, 1939. Russia agrees to withdraw from all territory west of a line running from Lake Ladoga south to Novgorod, south east to Vyazma to Voronezh on the Don River. The line then ran along the Don, to south of Tsaritsyn and toward the Caspian Sea. The entire Caucasus and Finland are occupied by German troops. These territories were reorganized by Germany. Romania annexed Bessarabia. In the Balkans Yugoslavia is partitioned between Germany, Italy, Hungary and Albania. Greece annexed Thrace from Bulgaria and is given the Dardanelles and Constantinople. Turkey annexed Russian Armenia. The British and French annex Russian territories in the Middle East and Persia. Mongolia is set up as a satellite state under Japanese

# WHAT IF BISMARCK HAD CREATED GREATER GERMANY INSTEAD OF LITTLE GERMANY?

## BY
### ROBERT BLUMETTI

This alternative history of the unification of Germany is actually an alternative time line based on two alternative turns of events. The first is what if Bismarck created a Greater German Reich instead of the smaller German Reich that excluded Austria. The second event concerns Prince Frederick, the son of Kaiser William I, who in my alternative history doesn't die from throat cancer in 1888.

In 1865 the Prussian Chancellor Otto von Bismarck set about ensuring the neutrality of Europe as a prelude to a war with Austria. Bismarck met with Napoleon III of France and promised the French Emperor that Prussian expansion would stop at the Main River, and Austria would be excluded from Germany. The two parts of Prussia would be united through the annexation of German-speaking territory, and a North German Confederation is subsequently founded under Bismarck's direction. Bismarck stressed the common interests of

Prussia and France in reorganizing Europe. Bismarck gave only vague promises to support French expansion toward the Rhine, in Belgium and Luxembourg. Bismarck was right in thinking he had ensured the neutrality of France. In light of these excellent Prusso-Russian relations and the immobility of Britain, only one thing remained to be done: Italy had to be ensnared into promising a second front to insure victory over Austria and her expected German allies.

# AUSTRO-PRUSSIAN WAR OF 1866

Bismarck deliberately forced a dispute between Prussia and Austria over the north German provinces of Schleswig and Holstein by making known his intentions to annex both provinces to Prussia. Prussia was the first to mobilize and although the Austrian army was numerically much larger, the Prussian army was better trained, better led, supplied, more aggressive, and equipped with the murderous needle gun. Prussia and Italy, her ally, were at war with Austria and most of the independent German states in the spring of 1866.

The Italian armies were defeated by the Austrians in June. The Austrians, however, were virtually knocked out of the war on July 3 in one of the biggest battles of the century—Sadowa. Despite the fact that the Austrians enjoyed the advantages of terrain and numbers (220,000 against 120,000 Prussians), the Austrians were defeated, suffers 45,000 deaths. With this victory, the Prussian army established its prestige over the civilian government. The way to Vienna was open and the victorious Prussians advanced towards the Hungarian border upon Vienna. Moltke and the Prussian general staff looked forward to a triumphal march through Austrian capital.

Bismarck had other plans. While the Prussian military and King William dreamed of extensive annexations in Bohemia and Saxony, Bismarck sought only to expel Austria from Germany. He objected to the continuation of the war and the conquest of Vienna. Heated arguments among Bismarck, the King of Prussia, and the General Staff arose. Bismarck threatened to retire if his plan for a limited victory was not accepted. The argument got so heated that at a conference Bismarck threatened to jump out a window if the King and the General Staff did not concur with him. The crown prince, Frederick, walked over to the window and opened it, and told Bismarck to jump. Bismarck was dumbfounded and backed down.

In our time line (OTL) Frederick sided with Bismarck.

Realizing that his bluff was called, Bismarck set about trying to prevent the war from escalating into a general European war. He sought to prevent the intervention of both Russia and France. The Prussian army brushed away all further Austrian resistance and entered Vienna. Emperor Joseph of Austria surrendered. In Hungary, the Hungarians rebelled in hope of establishing an independent Kingdom of Hungary. Russian armies were mobilized and rushed to the border of the Austrian Empire. Bismarck realized he had to act fast.

Bismarck contacted the Russians and invited them to occupy the Austrian province of Galicia, with the promise of supporting Russian claims to annexation. After Russia was defeated at the hands of Great Britain and France in the Crimean War, Russia was forbidden to maintain a naval presence on the Black Sea. Bismarck reassured the Tsar that he would support the Russian if they seek to remilitarize the Black Sea. In return, the Russians agreed not to invade Hungary and recognized the Greater German Reich. Bismarck next informed Napoleon III that he would support French annexation of Belgium or Luxemburg after the war. Napoleon agreed to Bismarck's demands. Everything now depended on the speed and adroitness with which he could negotiate a peace that would satisfy everyone and prevent the French and Russians from intervening.

# THE TREATY OF VIENNA

Since Bismarck's plans of creating a Kleinduetschland (small Germany) under Prussia's control was dashed, Bismarck had no other alternative but the creation of a Grossdeutschland, a great Germany. The Treaty of Vienna was signed on July 26. With this treaty, the Austrian Empire ceased to exist and was partitioned. Bismarck had not planned to declare the creation of a German Empire so soon, but the complete partition of Austria forced his hand. He tried to convince Wilhelm I that it was essential for him to accept the crown as German Emperor because he and the army created the present situation by their demands to completely defeat Austria. The King of Prussia, Wilhelm I wanted to be crowned the Emperor of Germany, but at the coronation in Vienna, Bismarck secretly arranged for everyone to shout 'Long Live the German Emperor'. Wilhelm I was helpless and reluctantly accepted the title, and was declared German Emperor in Vienna.

The Italians were permitted to annex not only Venetia, but the Italian inhabited areas of South Tyrol, Trieste, the Istian peninsula and the Dalmatian coast. Bismarck was true to his word to Russia. The Russian Empire annexed the Austrian province of Galicia, including the Polish city of Cracow. The Bukovina province was given to Turkey to prevent the Russians from annexing it. Hungary was set up as an independent kingdom, and Prince Leopold from southern Germany, Catholic house of Hohenzollern-Sigmaringen, which was related to King of Prussia, was crowned King of Hungary. The historical classes retained power in Hungary (the nobility and the clergy). In this way, Bismarck ensured an alliance between the new Prussian-led united Germany and Hungary.

Prussia annexed extensive territories in northern Germany, and King Wilhelm was crowned the German Emperor. The lesser states of the former German Confederation were included in the new German Empire. The Duchy of Bohemia was separated from Austria and made into a duchy. Emperor Francis Joseph of Austria was forced to abdicate, and his son, Rudolf was crowned the Grand Duke of the Grand Duchy of Austria, which included remainder of the Austrian territories and the territory of Burgenland. The Habsburgs were reduced in power and influence, and ceasing to be a rival of the Hohenzollerns for the leadership of Germany.

In the next several years the situation in Europe grew tense. The other powers of Europe were suddenly faced with a powerful, united Germany in the heart of Europe. Germany was clearly the most powerful country in Europe in 1869, possessing a population of 55,000,000, while the population of France was only 36,000,000. Napoleon III realized too late that he misjudged the power of Prussia. He thought Prussia would be defeated by Austria, or if Austria was defeated, Prussia would need the assistance of France to hammer out a treaty with Austria. Napoleon III never expected the total defeat of Austria, or her dismemberment. He was now faced with a united Germany that dominated central Europe.

Napoleon III immediately demanded the right for compensation in Western Europe, for France remaining neutral during the Austro-Prussian War. Bismarck had insinuated that France would be compensated with Luxembourg or Belgium. Now Napoleon III wanted his pound of flesh. His demands played right into Bismarck's hands. He was able to get Napoleon III to put his demands in writing, in a series of letters exchanged between the governments of France and Germany. Bismarck then used the dispatches to prove to Great Britain of French designs on the Low Lands. Bismarck next convinced the Russians that Germany would give Russia a free hand in the Balkans in a possible war between Germany and France. He assured the Czar that Germany had no interests beyond the Kingdom of Hungary. Once the Russians agreed not to intervene, Bismarck then sought Italian support by promising Italy could annex the French-occupied Papal State, which included the city of Rome, and the return of the lost provinces of Nice and Savoy. By 1870, Germany had isolated France.

# FRANCO-PRUSSIAN WAR OF 1970

Napoleon III's situation at home was becoming unsettled. His popularity was plummeting. Germany's unification had caused panic among the French. The people blamed Napoleon III for the debacle. Napoleon III felt he had to force Bismarck's hand on the issue of territorial compensation. In May 1870, France declared war on Germany.

Bismarck was prepared for the eventuality of war. The German General Staff had readied the German Reichwehr for war and quickly mobilized. The French Army was slow in mobilizing and was not ready when the German Army crossed the border and invaded France through Lorraine. The French were defeated at Metz and then at Verdun. The French Army made a last stand at Sedan. The Germans were victorious at the battle of Sedan, and Napoleon III was taken captive.

The Italians had mobilized along the French border, waiting for the opportunity to invade Savoy and Nice. The British had moved their fleet into the English Channel, fearing the possibility that the French might invade Belgium. In August 1870 as Napoleon III formally surrendered Paris exploded. Revolution broke out in Paris and the French Empire was overthrown. The rebels declared the formation of the Third French Republic, but refused to surrender to Germany. The German Army continued its advance and by October it had surrounded Paris. The capital was now under siege.

# THE TREATY OF PARIS AND THE CREATION OF THE GREATER GERMAN REICH

At first, the new government in Paris refused to surrender. The German army laid siege to Paris. After suffering through six months of siege, and a terrible winter, the new Republican government of France sued for peace. Bismarck terms were an indemnity of five billion dollars, German occupation of northeastern France until said amount was paid, and the German annexation of the provinces of Alsace-Lorraine, and Luxemburg. Bismarck supports the annexation of Savoy and Nice by Italy, hoping to create an open sore between the French and the Italians.

The creation of such a large German state caused problems for Bismarck. The new empire was actually a federal monarchy. The northern states, dominated by Prussia were Protestant, while the southern states were predominately Catholic. The population of Germany was 50% Protestant and 50% Catholic. Bismarck

had to find a way to keep peace between the two religions. While he feared inter-
ference by the Catholic Church in German politics, he had to be careful not to
cause a cultural war with the Catholic south. Any struggle between the protestant
north and the Catholic south could only strengthen the Habsburg dynasty within
the new German Empire. The weak spot among the Catholic states was the large
Czech population in the Duchy of Bohemia. He pushed through a Germanization program that antagonized the Slavic populations, as well as the eastern
regions of Prussia with their large Polish population. Slavic reaction helped to
unify the German Catholics and Protestants in a campaign of German nationalism. The German Catholic Church was divided because the Poles and Czechs
were also both Catholic, but many German Catholics resented the Catholic
Church's opposition of Bismarck's anti-Slavic policy.

# THE BISMARCKIAN SYSTEM

In OTL Germany's population was only about one-third Catholic. Bismarck's
Kulturkampf was designed to attack the Catholic Church and prevent it from
developing into a powerful voice in German politics.

Bismarck also feared the rise of socialism within the new German Empire.
Germany was rapidly industrializing during the 1870s and 1880s. This resulted
in a rapidly-growing proletariat. To prevent the radicalization of German workers, Bismarck passed a series of reform programs designed to help the working
class, including the first social security program in Europe. This policy came to be
known as Social Prussianism.

Fearing the French would seek revenge and upset the peace of Europe, Bismarck begins to build a network of alliances in order to isolate France. He forms
a Quadruple Alliance with Hungary, Russia and Italy. Since Hungary, Italy and
Russia have no conflicting interests, and Bismarck supports Russian interests in
the Balkans, this alliance proves to be stabile. Italy fears the French will seek to
retake Savoy and Nice and so supports Germany. Italy hopes to acquire Corsica
and is angry when the French annex the African territory of Tunisia.

Under German influence, Hungary is neither expansionist, nor does the King
of Hungary have any interest in annexing Bosnia. When Serbia rebels against
Turkey, Russia supports the Serbs. In 1878 Russia goes to war with Turkey,
defeating the Turks. Britain threatens to intervene, but Bismarck prevents a
European war by convening a Congress in Berlin. The British are permitted to
control the straits between the Aegen Sea and the Black Sea, and prevent the Russians from occupying Constantinople. But the Russians are able to create an inde-

pendent Bulgaria that includes Macedonia, and an independent Serbia that includes Bosnia. Both the Russians and the British are pleased.

# FREDERICK III BECOMES KAISER OF GERMANY IN 1888

Kaiser Wilhelm I dies in 1888 and his son is crown Frederick III. In OTL Frederick dies of throat cancer several months later, but in this time line he doesn't have cancer and lives. In OTL Wilhelm II becomes Kaiser and forces Bismarck to resign in 1890. Wilhelm II then lets Germany's alliance with Russia elapse and begins a program of naval construction that antagonizes Great Britain. But in this time line, Frederick III's wife, who is the eldest daughter of Great Britain's Queen Victoria, convinces the new German Kaiser to seek closer relations with Great Britain. In 1892, Frederick III does not renew the Quadruple Alliance with Russia. Frederick III advocates reforms that gradually move Germany toward a constitutional monarchy modeled after England. Though Bismarck opposes Frederick III's liberalization programs, the Kaiser is forced to keep Bismarck as chancellor, in order to him stop the growing influence of the naval lobby.

Both Frederick III and Bismarck oppose Germany entering into a scramble for overseas colonies, and support a conservative, European-based policy. Together they are successful in preventing the naval lobby's plans for the creation of a large German navy, and the quest for overseas colonies. The British are pleased with Germany's policy and Bismarck is able to negotiate several treaties that exchange Germany's small holdings in East Africa, for Heligoland island off the coast of Germany. Frederick III and Bismarck negotiate a trade agreement with Great Britain. Germany agrees to sell all her African holdings—Togo, Cameroon, German East Africa and German Southwest Africa, in return for Great Britain granting most-favored status to German businesses. Germany's businesses are granted the right to trade freely throughout the British Empire.

Bismarck fears that France will seek an alliance with Russia now that his alliance with Russia was not renewed. He secretly enters into negotiations with the Russians and convinces the Kaiser to agree to a secret Reassurance Treaty between Germany and Russia. It was a non-aggression treaty in which both nations agreed to remain neutral if either nation goes to war against a third power.

Through the 1890s Britain, France and Russia continue their quest for new colonies in Asia and Africa. Frederick III and Bismarck wisely contain those elements within German society who wish to acquire overseas colonies. As Britain finds herself pitted against French expansion in northeast Africa and Russian expansion in central Asia, British leaders seek closer relations with Germany. In 1894 Bismarck signs the Anglo-German Entente. In the Entente treaty both countries agree not to go to war against the other, and remain neutral if either country finds itself at war with a third power. Germany also agrees to restrict her navy's growth. In return, Britain promises to protect the German coast if Germany finds herself at war with a third power. Since the only powers that could possibly represent a threat to the German coast in the North Sea or the Baltic Sea are France and Russia, Britain was actually promising to come to Germany's defense if attacked by either power.

Britain also signs treaties with Italy and Hungary to win favor with Germany. When Italy invades Abyssinia in 1895, Britain withholds support for the Africans. Italy defeats the Abyssinians and annexe Abyssinia to the Italian Empire.

## THE POST BISMARCKIAN SYSTEM

Otto von Bismarck dies in 1898. He is given a state funeral and declared a national hero. In 1902 his Reassurance Treaty with Russia is not renewed. Though relations between Russia and Germany remain good, the French begin to seek closer relations with Russia due to their shared rivalries with Great Britain.

In 1894 Japan attacked China defeating the celestial empire. Japan annexe Formosa and the Pescadores Islands, and forces China to surrender Port Arthur, and the southern section of Manchuria linking the port with Japanese-controlled Korea. Japan then receives the remainder of Manchuria as part of its sphere of influence. Russia and France protest, but Japan ignores them. Tensions among Japan and France and Russia grow over the next six years. In 1904 Russia and France signed the Dual Alliance. Both nations agree to come to the other's defense if either finds itself at war with a third power. France hopes to draw Russia into a war with Germany, and Russia hoped to draw France into a war with Japan. Both nations promises to work together against British imperialism. But as tensions between the Russians and the Japanese in Manchuria escalate, the Japanese declare war on Russia in 1905. France immediately declares war on Japan.

The Japanese are able to quickly defeat the Russians when Russia tries to invade Korea. When the Japanese invade Manchuria, they are forced to call off the invasion when a combined Franco-Russian fleet appears in the Yellow Sea and defeats the Japanese fleet off the coast of Port Arthur. The war is a draw with Japanese victories on land and France and Russia victories at sea. With the lost of the Japanese fleet, Japan is unable to continue the war on the Asian mainland. President Theodore Roosevelt agrees to mediate among the warring nations. Japan is permitted to retain Korea and Port Arthur, but has to evacuate southern Manchuria. Russia is permitted to annex northern Manchuria and occupy southern Manchuria as its sphere of influence. France is permitted to annex the Chinese city of Kiaochow and given the Shantung peninsula as its sphere of influence. Japan is smarting from the defeat and signs an alliance with Great Britain in 1906.

# THE BALKAN CRISIS OF 1908-1909

The decay of the Ottoman Empire contributes to unrest in the Balkans. National, ethnic and religious divisions keep the Balkans in a constant state of conflict. In 1908 a group called the Young Turks rebelles and attempt to transform the Ottoman Empire into a modern state. Albanians still under Turkish control rebel and seek independence. The Serbs seek to annex Albania. The Turks are willing to grant independence to the Albanians but warn the Serbs not to interfere. Russia backs the Serbs, but Britain supports the Turks. Germany, Hungary, and Italy all support Britain, while France supports Russia. The Bulgarians support Serbia, but Romania, fearing Russian expansion at her expanse, supports Turkey. Greece remains neutral. The dispute continues to fester throughout the winter and civil war rages in Bosnia.

In the Spring of 1909 Great Britain stationed her fleet in the Straits of the Bosporus and the Dardanelles, closing them to the Russian fleet. The Russians send the Turks an ultimatum, demanding the Turks withdraw from Bosnia. The Turks refuses and askes for Britain's support. The British agree. The French promise to support their Russian allies, while Frederick III of Germany promises the British they can count on German support in the advent of war.

The Russians announce the mobilization of their armies in April 1909 and declare war on Turkey. Great Britain declares war on Russia, and France declares war on Britain. Count Alfred von Schlieffen, the head of the German General Staff has planned for the eventuality of Germany fighting a two-front war with France and Russia. On May 12, 1909, Germany informed the Belgium government of it intend to move through it in an attack on France. At first King Leopold of Belgium refuses to permit the Germans to pass through his country, but after the English King informs him that Great Britain would support the Germans, Leopold agrees.

# THE GERMAN INVASION OF FRANCE

Von Schlieffen's plan called for a defensive war in the east against Russia. In the west, a quick decision was sought, through the encirclement of the French army by a strong right-wing. As the French attacked Germany through Alsace-Lorraine, the German seventh army pulled back drawing the French into Germany. At the same time, six German armies raced unopposed through Belgium and into northern France. The British fleet bombed the French ports of Dunkirk, Calais, and Boulogne, landing the British Expeditionary Force to occupy these ports. The German army easily swung west of Paris, encircling the French capital and proceeded to crush the French army in the Battle of the Seine, June 26-29. The French government sued for peace on July 14.

With the defeat of the French, von Schlieffen sent three armies east. The Russians invaded both East Prussia and Romania. Generals Hindenburg and Ludendorff were able to devise a plan in which the German army encircled the Russians in the Battle of Tannenberg, in East Prussia. With the defeat of the Russian army, the Germans invade Russia. All along the Eastern Front the Germans and their allies counter attacked. By July 15 they had occupied Poland, Galicia, Lithuania and Courland and invaded Bessarabia, while the British fleet attacked and destroyed the Russian fleet in the Black Sea. In the Far East, the Japanese invade Southern Manchuria. The Russians sued for peace on August 13.

# THE TREATY OF VIENNA OF 1910

The great powers of Europe met in Vienna and signed a peace treaty in 1910. Under the treaty Germany annexed the French territories of Belfort, Longwy and Etain, as well as the Duchy of Luxembourg. Belgium was given Revin and Lille for permitting the German army's passage through its territory. Germany annexed some Polish territory and Lithuania. Independent states in Poland, Latvia, Estonia and Finland were created and allied to Germany. Romania received Bessarabia from Russia and Dobrudja from Bulgaria. Turkey received the Caucasus from Russia and Tabriz from Persia. The Black Sea was demilitarized. Bulgaria lost Eastern Roumelia to Turkey. Bosnia was made into a independent kingdom.

In the Far East, Japan annexed Southern Manchuria, Northern Sakhalin Island and the French port of Tsingtao in China.

In Africa the Germans annexed the French colonies of the French Equatorial Africa, Gabon and Morocco.

The Italians annexed Tunisia and Djibouti in Africa, as well as Savoy and Nice in Europe. Corsica was made an independent state under Italian jurisdiction.

The British annexed Madagascar, Southern Persia, Tibet and received Northern Persia as a protectore. The French Islands of Comoro, Reunion, St. Paul and Kerguelen in the Indian Ocean were annexed, as well as the French ports of Yanaon, Mahe, Pondicherry and Karikal on the Indian subcontinent. The British also annexed the French possessions of New Hebrides, New Caledonia, the Marquesas, Society islands and the Tuamotu Archipelago in the Pacific Ocean.

# DOOMED AT D-DAY

# WHAT IF THE ALLIES WERE DEFEATED AT NORMANDY IN JUNE, 1944?

## THE INVASION OF NORMANDY

With the allied invasion of France at Normandy was the Germans lost its last opportunity to prevent a military defeat in World War Two. Even if Germany had driven the Allies back into the sea at Normandy, Germany would not have won the war against the United States, yet Germany could have achieved a negotiated settlement to end the war. Hitler anticipated the invasion of France. In December 1943 he said: "If they attack in the West, the attack will decide the war." If the Allies could be thrown back into the sea, they could not mount another invasion for at least another year, and maybe up to eighteen months, if ever. Hitler would be free to transfer most of his fifty-nine divisions, including ten panzer divisions, to the East for a showdown with the Soviet Union. This is how it could have happened.

Before the invasion, the German military was split on how to face the eventual Allied invasion that they knew was coming. Field Marshal Rundstedt, who was in charge of the defense of Western Europe, believed the best way to defeat the Allies was to station German panzer divisions in the interior and wait for the Allies to establish a beach head. Once they began to drive inland, the panzer divisions should then be moved forward in concentrated force, and engage the Allied forces driving them back into the sea. Under Rundstedt was Field Marshal Rommel, the Desert Fox. Rommel felt that it would be impractical to hold the panzer divisions back because of Allied air superiority. With complete control of the air, the Allied air force would destroy the panzer divisions as they were moving forward. He felt the best way to counter Allied air superiority was to position panzer divisions close enough to the coast to knock the Allied invasion force out just as they were trying to establish their beachheads.

The Germans realized that there were only two likely locations in where the Allies could possibly invade France. The first was Calais and the second was Normandy. Rommel realized this and concentrated on fortifying these two locations. In May 1944, Hitler had a premonition that the invasion would come at Normandy and ordered the reinforcement of German defense there. Rommel wanted to move the three panzer divisions stationed there, the Lehr Panzer, the 21 Panzer and the 12 SS Panzer. Rommel wanted to move them to the coast, but Rundsedt refused. Rommel went over Rundsedt head directly to Hitler. Hitler compromised by permitting Rommel to move the 12 SS Panzer forward. Ironically, of the five beachheads that the Allies established on June 6, the only one in which they were almost driven back into the sea, was at Omaha Beach where the 12 SS Panzer division was stationed. What would have happened if all three panzer divisions were moved to the coast as Rommel wanted?

In this Alternative Time Line (ATL) Rommel convinces Hitler to move the panzer divisions close to the coast. He also convinced Hitler to hold the V-1 rockets in reserve for a concentrated assault against the south of England once the invasion began. This would have disrupted the invasion force setting out to Normandy.

Once the invasion began on the morning of June 6, the German Generals thought it a diversion and refused to wake Hitler. When Hitler was finally waken, he was convinced that it was a decoy and the real invasion would come at Calais. He hesitated to send reinforcements to Normandy. What would have happened if he was awakened and had sent reinforcements to help the three panzer divisions already stationed at Normandy?

On June 6, 1944, the Anglo-American invasion fleet began landing all along the coast at Normandy at 0500 hours. Eisenhower had assembled an impressive force of 150,000 men, 1,500 tanks, 5,300 ships and 12,000 aircraft. A successful invasion depended upon this enormous Allied air superiority—a ratio of 30 to 1.

German military intelligence reports of the landings to German military command and determined that Normandy was the main invasion site. Field Marshal von Rundstedt decided to ignore many of his generals who believe the Normandy invasion was just a diversion. He summons the courage to wake Hitler and inform him of the landings and his opinion that this is the real invasion. By 0600 hours Hitler is convinced that the Normandy landings are the long-waited-for invasion, and orders reinforcements rushed to the coast.

The Allies quickly establish control of the air and begin attacking German forces rushing to the coast, but the three panzer divisions that are already stationed close to the coast, where the Allies were trying to establish five beachheads, are already attacking the landing forces. The Allies are slaughtered as they tried to establish their beachheads. Their ships began bombarding the German forces from the sea, but by 0900 German reinforcements were able to reach the coast. By 1300 hours, the Allies were thrown back into the sea at the Omaha and Utah beaches. By 1500 hours the Allied troops had to evacuate the coast despite their air superiority. Over fifty thousand German troops had reached the coast to support the three panzer divisions. By 1900 hours the Germans had reestablished control of the entire coast once again.

The British newspapers of June 7 referred to the failed invasion as a second Dunkirk. Most of the Allied troops had escaped with their lives, but most of the heavy equipment was lost on the beaches. At 1000 hours General Eisenhower issues prepared statement to the press after sending it to Roosevelt and all Allied military leaders. "Our landings in the Cherbourg Havre area have failed to gain a satisfactory foothold and I have withdrawn the troops. My decision to attack at this time and place was based upon the best information available. The troops, the air and the navy did all that bravery and devotion to duty could do. If any blame or fault attaches to the attempt it is mine alone." The defeat undermines the British self-confidence more than it does than the Americans. Britain was exhausted from five years of war. The British High Command had opposed the invasion, preferring to guard its last reserves of manpower. By May 1944, British strength peaked at 2.75 million men. Bu comparison, the American armed forces included 5.75 million and was still growing. From this point on, British strength began decreasing. If the invasion had succeeded, the British could have sent another two additional armies to the continent, one of them being Canadian and no more. Britain had no desire to risk its status as a world power by exhausting the last of its reserves in a war of attrition in France. Churchill had preferred to continue the assault on Italy or invade the Balkans. But the Americans had their way, and the Allied invasion of France failed. Britain is now demoralized.

# THE BRITISH AGREE TO PEACE WITH GERMANY

On June 8, Hitler sends an offer of peace to the British government. He hopes to divide the British from the Americans and proposes generous terms. Churchill refuses to consider the peace proposal, but his government is divided. Word of the peace proposal is leaked by members of the Labor Party in House of Commons. On June 12 Clement R. Attlee, leader of the Labor Party, announces the withdrawal of the Labor Party from the national government and calls for Churchill's resignation. The British economy is on its last leg, and is only maintained by generous aid from the Americans. The demoralized British and fear that the war will last another two years. The demands for peace spread throughout Great Britain. Churchill is forced to resign as Prime Minister on June 18. He is replaced by Lord Halifax, who says in Parliament, "We have fought honorably and heroically, but now we must face the truth that we are exhausted. We must put an end to this war now, and seek an honorable peace that will permit our institutions to survive and ensure the survival of the British Empire. Our only hope lies in a system of peaceful coexistence with Germany."

Halifax informs the U.S. government that Britain has decided to withdraw from the war. Negotiations between Britain and Germany open immediately and a hastily drawn-up agreement is arrived at. The agreement calls for an end to all hostilities, the withdrawal of all hostile (American) forces from British soil, the acceptance of current borders, no reparations and Britain and Germany agree to work together in a new system of peaceful coexistence.

Prime Minister Halifax agrees to sign an armistice with Japan. Britain agrees to surrender all claims to Hong Kong, Burma, Malaysia, Singapore and other British territories under Japanese control. In return, India is retained by Britain. Australia and New Zealand refuse to sign the treaty and both governments announced their secession from the British Commonwealth and Empire. After the United States gave both governments its reassurance of American support to continue the war against Japan, Australia and New Zealand sign military alliances with the United States.

On June 27 British Fascist leader Sir Oswald Mosley announces he is reforming the British Union of Fascist under a new name, the British Fascist Party. He plans to run candidates in the next parliamentary elections and declares his support for a new era of Anglo-German friendship and cooperation.

President Roosevelt is furious at the British. He wanted to continue the war against Germany, but after the British demand that the Americans withdraw from Great Britain the American military concluded that it would be impossible to mount another invasion of Europe. On June 22, 1944, Winston Churchill and his family leave Britain for the United States. They will never return and become American citizens.

# THE UNITED STATES DECIDES TO CONTINUE THE WAR AGAINST GERMANY

General Marshal, after being pressured by the majority of the military leaders of the U.S. Armed Forces, is convinced that the best course of attack is to continue the war against Germany, but shift the American war effort to the war against Japan in the Pacific. Roosevelt and most of the cabinet is forced to agree. Yet, there is no way the United States could continue to conduct its war against Germany from Italy and French North Africa. The United States could not possibly continue its massive bombing of German cities from Italy and North Africa. At best, the American leaders hope to tie down as many German divisions as possible while the Soviet continue their offensive against Germany. Marshal and Roosevelt, were sure the U.S. could develop the atomic bomb in the next year, and plan to use it against Germany and Japan, in the hope of bringing the war to a victorious conclusion.

As the British withdrew from Italy, German troops are ready to mount an attack through the gaps in the front. By August, the United States is forced to withdraw from Italy. The Germans were able to reoccupy all of Italy, except for Sicily. Mussolini's Social Fascist Republic returns to Rome, but he has to agree to the loss of the northern half of South Tyrol and Trieste and Fiume by Germany. The Italian King is forced to abdicate, deposing the Italian monarchy. Over the next three months, Americans are entrenched in Sicily and North Africa. All U-boat activities in the Atlantic shifted to the western Atlantic. Germany now put pressure on Spain, and Franco announces that he will permit German U-boats to operate from Spanish ports. This makes it difficult for the United States to continue to supply its troops in Sicily and North Africa.

# ROOSEVELT DIES

On July 1, Roosevelt in a radio address informs the American people of the end of the war in Europe, but encourages them to continue the struggle with Japan. "More than ever we need to continue to fight to victory in the Pacific if our liberty and Republic are to survive." Roosevelt suffers a stroke on July 3. FDR had suffered from poor health over the last three years. Throughout 1942 and 1943 he suffered attacks of grippe and fevers of 104 degrees. He also suffered from respiratory problems, especially when he was under stress. He is tormented by headaches throughout 1943 and 1944. They continue to get worse and he has trouble concentrating. His pallor was gray and his hands trembled so badly that he could not shave himself. It was discovered that FDR's heart was enlarged and there was blue tinge on his lips and fingernails caused by fluid in his lungs. His blood pressure was 186/108. On this depressed, dying man the American government and military had pinned all their hopes to continue their global war. But it was not to be. On July 15, Roosevelt suffers another heart attack and dies from congestive heart failure. Henry Wallace is sworn in as President of the United States. Wallace agrees to continue to persecute war against Germany.

# THE GERMAN SUMMER OFFENSIVE AGAINST THE SOVIET UNION IN 1944

With the defeat at Normandy and the withdrawal of Great Britain from the war in Europe, Stalin decides to postpone the planned Soviet summer offensive planned for June 22, 1944. The German armed forces include 59 divisions in France, 23 divisions in Italy and 163 divisions facing the Soviets. Now that the war in the West is over, Hitler reassigns 60 divisions from France and Italy to the Eastern Front. At the same time, Himmler continues to recruit non-Germans into the Waffen SS. With the cessation of lend-lease aid from the United States, Stalin knew that a long war with Germany could still be lost. Stalin tried to open negotiations with Germany, but Hitler refuses. He still dreams of an eastern empire reaching to the Urals. When Stalin decides to resume the attack on August 22, the Germans are prepared for the attack.

    The Soviet attack begins against German Army Group Center. Two pincer movements from Vitebsk and Bobruisk attack. Their objective is to take Minsk. The German forces were waiting for the Soviets spearheads. The additional divisions, plus the arrival of the new Ms 262 jet fighters and V-1 rockets help Rommel and Guderian, under von Manstein's command, to destroy the Soviet pincers. Relying on the time proven tactic of permitting the Soviets to drive deep into German lines then attack at the flanks of the Soviet advancing forces. The result was the death and capture of 550,000 Soviet troops. Stalin is forced to call off the Soviet offensive. News of this victory spread, throughout Germany revitalizing the nation's moral.

With this defeat of the Soviet summer offensive, Hitler demands that the Wehrmarcht go on the offensive in the Ukraine. News of the German victory helps to fortify the resolve of Germany's allies in Hungary, Romania and Finland. In September 1944 the Germans try to reproduce their Kiev offensive of 1941. Panzer armies sweep south toward Kiev from the north while Army Group South attacks from Romania. Stalin orders a retreat. The Soviets manage to withdraw beyond the Dnieper River, but over 200,000 Soviet troops are captured before they can escape. The Germans continue their advance through the Ukraine pushing Soviet forces back to the Dnieper River.

# THE REPUBLICANS WIN IN 1944

On June 26-29 1944, the Republican Party holds its national convention in Chicago. The Republicans nominate Governor Thomas E. Dewey of New York for president and Governor John W. Bricker of Ohio for vice president. Bricker is a conservative and an isolationist. Dewey and Bricker promise to continue the war against the Japanese, but seek peaceful coexistence with the New Order in Europe.

With FDR's death, the Democratic Party is split between leftist New Dealers and conservative Southern Democrats. In 1942, the GOP captures the governorship of both New Jersey and Kentucky. Pennsylvania, Connecticut and California go heavily Republican in local elections. The GOP now controls twenty-six states with a total electoral college vote of 342. While the GOP is united, the two different wings of the Democratic Party were at each other throats. Fratricide was wrecking the Democratic Party. Polls taken in 1943 showed that FDR would have won the election with 51 percent, but they also showed that he would have lost by 51 to 30 percent if the war would end by election day, 1944.

The Democrats also met in Chicago in July and after fifty-seven ballots, they nominated Vice-President Henry Wallace for president. The Democratic Party is badly split. The Southerners oppose Wallace's leftist polices, especially his support for civil rights for blacks. Wallace campaigns on the promise he will increase aid and support for the Soviet Union. Wallace also promises to continue the war on Germany if he is elected president. The American people never really felt the same hostility toward the Germans as they did against the Japanese. They hated the Japanese because of the attack on Pearl Harbor, in addition to the fact that the Japanese are a yellow race, while the Germans are white. Most people felt the war in Europe was over and wanted to concentrate on defeating Japan. Top military brass also began pushing for an armistice with Germany and making the war against Japan the first priority of America's war effort.

Robert Hannegan, Chairman of the Democratic party, Bronx boss Ed Flynn and Mayor Ed Kelly of Chicago, as well as Postmaster General Frank Walker organize the effort to stop Wallace's nomination at the Democratic convention. But Wallace is able to out maneuver them by personally appearing at the convention and speaking to the delegation. He is able to win over the convention hall securing the nomination. After Wallace's nomination, the Southerners walk out of the convention. During the campaign, Wallace is denounced by Southern democrats as a Communist. Wallace's popularity plummets.

In September of 1944, General MacArthur announces his return when U.S. forces land on Leyte in the Philippines. The Battle of the Philippines results in the destruction of most of what is left of the Japanese navy.

# HITLER'S NEW ORDER IN EUROPE

In September 1944, Hitler holds a conference in Berlin. Leaders from across German dominated Europe sign the New Order Alliance. Included are the newly installed fascist governments of Hungary and Romania. Generalissimo Franco is also present and announces Spain's entrance into the war against Russia and Communism. The newly reunified government of France is also present. Minister Laval announces that France would send troops to fight against Communism on the Eastern Front. Germany officially annexes the Netherlands and Belgium, as well as a strip of French territory running from Flanders to Switzerland.

By November 1944, the Germans begin the long process of rebuilding. With the cessation of Anglo-American bombing of German cities, Albert Speer, who was able to increase German production even under the worst of wartime conditions, was able to perform an economic miracle. German cities are rapidly rebuilt. Production of tanks and aircraft, including the new Ms 262 and He 178 jet fighters, increase rapidly. V-2 rockets are launched against Soviet forces on the Eastern front. Goering announces the production of a new flying-wing jet-bomber that will be able to reach Soviet industrial centers beyond the Ural Mountains. He promises the first jet-bombers by spring of 1945.

Stalin decides to occupy all of Persia. Soviet troops invade the southern half of Persia. British troops station fire upon the Soviets, but are unable to stop them. Britain request German assistance. On November 16 Prime Minister Halifax joins Germany's New Order Alliance. Turkey soon follows suit joining the alliance. German troops are rushed through Turkey into Iraq. On December 5 a joint German-British-Turkish army invades Persia. The Persians rise in rebellion against the Soviets. Germany now has ample supplies of Middle eastern oil. The oil fields in the Soviet Caucasus are within striking distance of a German forces.

Reichfuehrer Himmler continues to enlarge the number of Waffen SS divisions. He is now able to recruit large numbers of Europeans from France, Italy, the Low Countries, Scandinavia and the Balkans. By December 1945 the Waffen SS has fifty-one divisions.

## DEWEY WINS

On November 7, Thomas E. Dewey is elected President of the United States by a landslide. He receives 63% of the vote. The Republicans are able to capture control of both houses of Congress. Charles Lindbergh is also elected to the U.S. Senate. The Republican Party is dominated by two factions; the Eastern big business elite and by Mid-Western isolationists. These two factions formed an alliance in the Dewey-Bricker ticket. President Dewey promises to seek an armistice with Germany, but continue to fight on to victory in the Pacific. The Democratic Party is seriously damaged. The Southerners revolted against the party and backed Dewey for President. The Republican leaders hoped to keep them within the Republican Party by promising to maintain segregation in the South. Jewish financial support for the Democratic Party in 1944 was seen by elements on the American political right as a Jewish-Communist conspiracy to drag America into the war in Europe with Germany again.

## THE UNITED STATES AND GERMANY SIGN A PEACE TREATY

General Marshal, pressured by the majority of the American military leaders was convinced that the best course was to conclude an armistice in Europe while continuing the war against Japan to a victorious conclusion. Marshal confronted Wallace with the situation of lack of support of the Armed Forces for continuing the war in Europe, and convinced him to open talks with the Germans. On November 20, German and American officers met under a flag-of-truce in the Vatican City, to discuss terms for a peace treaty.

The Treaty of Rome is signed on December 24 and is popularly know as the Christmas Treaty. The United States agrees to withdraw from Sicily, permitting the island to be occupied by Mussolini's Social Fascist Republic. Over the next three months, American troops withdraw from North Africa, and all U-boat activities in the Atlantic cease. Germany agrees to abandon support to Japan, and the United States agrees to terminate all military and economic aid to the Soviet Union. A small contingent of German and Italian troops re-occupy Libya in August, and Italian East Africa (Somalia, Eritrea and Ethiopia), forcing Emperor Haile Selassie to flee for a second time in ten years.

On January 20 1945, Dewey is sworn in as President of the United States. He announces that the United States will hold talks with Germany to reestablish diplomatic relations. Dewey appoints John F. Dulles as his Secretary of State. Dulles is pro-German and hopes to improve relations with the new German-dominated Europe. Dewey promises to work to undo many New Deal programs and urges the nation to unite for victory over Japan. He tells the American people that their destiny lies in the Pacific. Dewey plans to build a new political alliance among big business, Mid-Western populists, and Southern segregationists.

N the Pacific, the American offensive against Japan continue, and on February 1 1945 the American flag is raised over the island of Iwo Jima.

# GERMAN SPRING OFFENSIVE AGAINST THE SOVIET UNION

In March 1945, Sweden and Switzerland both announce they will join Germany's New Order.

On April 10 1945, the Germans unleash Operation Frederick. Army Group South strikes from the Ukraine and takes Kiev and the Donets Basin. At the same time a German-Turkish force strikes north in the Caucasus. The Germans can now establish air supremacy with thousands of new jet fighters at its command. The first long-range flying-wing jet-bombers begin striking at Soviet industries. Soviets cities are now subject to the same type of relentless, round-the-clocking bombing that German cities endured less than a year earlier. Within the next five months Moscow, Gorki, Kasan, Simbrisk, Orenburg, Saratov, and Ufa are reduced to rubbles. German troops sweep through the Caucasus and link up at Mount Elbruz. In the north, the Germans and Finns take Leningrad in August

1945. The new two-stage, V-3 rockets are also launched. They have a range of two thousand miles.

In June 1945 German Foreign Minster von Ribbentrop and Secretary of State Dulles meet in Washington to negotiate the Mutual-Assurance Treaty between Germany and the United States. It is agreed that the entire Western Hemisphere, and the Pacific Ocean and Far East are American spheres' of influence while Europe, Africa and Western Asia are Germany spheres' of influence. Both nations agree to trade arrangements and the demilitarization of the Atlantic. The treaties are hotly debated in Congress. The left-wing of the Democratic Party opposes the treaties. Jewish groups in America try to stir-up anti-Nazi hysteria. Opposition from isolationist forces, led by Senator Lindbergh, work for passage of the treaties. Finally, the Southern Democrats bolt from the Democratic Party and support the treaties. They are alienated by the Democratic left-wing's support for civil rights for blacks. German-American groups that are pro-Hitler begin to grow in strength.

# THE UNITED STATES DEFEATS JAPAN

On July 16 the United States explodes the first atomic bomb in Alamogordo, New Mexico. President Dewey gives the go ahead to drop two bombs on Japan. The first is dropped on Hiroshima on August 6 and the second on Nagasaki three days later. The Emperor of Japan agrees to the unconditional surrender of Japan one week later. By the end of August U.S. troops begin occupying Japan. MacArthur becomes the Military Governor of Japan. President Dewey abandons support for the United Nations.

The Pacific Alliance is signed by the United States, Australia and New Zealand on August 30. Many of the British islands in the Pacific Ocean were occupied by the United States during the war. Britain agreed to surrender these islands to the United States as part of the treaty signed between Germany and the United States in 1944.

American troops occupy all of Korea. There are border disputes and incidents between the American troops and the Chinese Communists who dominate Manchuria. President Dewey meets with Chiang Kai-shek in Hawaii on September 14. President Dewey promises to arm and support the Chinese Nationalist government and encourages Chiang to attack the Communist in northern China.

# THE SOVIET UNION COLLAPSE

On August 18, 1945, Moscow falls to the Germans. Stalin and the Soviet government are forced to flee to Siberia. Leningrad falls to the Germans on August 29 and the Germans quickly sweep into the Caucasus. German rockets and the long-range jet bomber, the Horten flying wing, rains terror and destruction on the Russian cities east of the Volga river and beyond the Ural mountains. General Georgi Zhukov leads a military putsch against Stalin, killing him along with Molotov, Kaganovich, Beria, and other leading Communist officials. Khukov forms the new Russian Federal Republic and opens talks with the German government on September 5. It is agreed that all Soviet forces must withdraw east of the Ural Mountains.

When Hitler receives the new that the Americans dropped two atomic bombs on Japan, he was furious. The magnitude of the atomic bomb's destructive power was not lost on Hitler. He realized that the United States suddenly obtained an instant strategic superiority over Germany. Hitler had been told by Professor Werner Heisenberg in 1942 that an atomic bomb could not be developed for another ten years. Hitler calls a meeting with the top atomic scientists in Europe. Doctor Heisenberg, Professor Otto Han, Professor Paul Harteck, Doctor Kurt Diebner and other German scientists were shocked that the Americans actually built and used the bomb on Japan. When Hitler berated his scientists for their unwillingness to work on Germany's behalf to develop a german atomic bomb. He promises to put at their disposal whatever resources necessary for them to develop an atomic bomb, warning them of the price of their failure. Heisenberg understood all too well what Hitler meant. Albert Speer was put in charge of Germany's effort to build a German atomic bomb, and it is called Project Thor's Hammer. Himmler had wanted the project to be placed under SS jurisdiction, but Hitler over rules him for he knew that if anyone could build the bomb in as short a time as possible it was Speer.

# POLITICAL POLARIZATION IN THE UNITED STATES

In the United States, Henry Wallace and other left-wing Democrats, as well as Jewish groups demand that the United States declare war on Germany and drop the atomic bomb on Berlin. But the American people having had enough of the war, seek a return to normalcy. In September 1945, the Left in America organize demonstrations charging that there are Nazis in the United States government.

They also blame the defeat of the Soviet Union on an U.S.-Nazi conspiracy. German-American groups, isolationist groups, American nationalists and Southern segregationists all counter-demonstrate.

In January 1946 Admiral E. Kimmel, the former commander-in-chief of the U.S. Pacific Fleet in 1941 and Lieutenant General Walter Short, the commanders of U.S. ground forces in Hawaii in 1941 are supported by Senator Lindbergh and Senator Arthur Vandenberg and both call for a complete investigation into the bombing of Pearl Harbor. The Congress hold committee meetings and investigate the events leading up to Pearl Harbor. President Dewey makes available secret communications and minutes from FDR's oval office. An exhaustive investigation concludes that there is hard evidence that FDR and members of his cabinet were involved in a conspiracy from 1939 to 1941 whose aim was to bring America into the war against Germany It is also revealed that Roosevelt deliberately maneuvered Japan into activities that resulted the attack on Pearl Harbor, after he failed to force Germany into declaring war on the United States by attacking German U-boats in the North Atlantic in 1941.

The American people are outraged. Cordell Hull, Henry Morgenthau, George Marshal, and many other members of the Roosevelt administration are drilled before the Congress. After three months, charges of treason are brought against over fifty people, including Generals Marshal and Eisenhower. Admiral Kimmel and General Short, former commanders of the U.S. Pacific Fleet in 1941, and commander of U.S. ground forces in Hawaii, are cleared of all charges. Demonstrations erupt throughout America and many of them become violent and anti-Semitic in nature.

Frightened by the anger and violence, atomic scientist, Enrico Fermi comes forward charging that Dr. Oppenheimer and other scientists who worked on the Manhattan Project are guilty of sending atomic secrets to the Soviet Union in July 1946. The Congressional committee now turns its attention to the Manhattan Project. Once again it is discovered that many of the scientists were guilty of espionage on behalf of the Soviet Union, sending atomic secrets to Communists. Dr. Oppenheimer, as well as a dozen other people who were involved in the Manhattan Project are also brought up on charges of treason. Even Albert Einstein falls under suspicion. Pro-Nazi and white nationalists groups exploit the fact that all the atomic scientists found guilty are Jewish. An anti-Semitic campaign is unleashed in the United States throughout 1946.

FBI director, J. Edgar Hoover announces that his agency has discovered that Congressman Dickstein of New York has been on the payroll of the Soviet Union for over ten years. Dickstein is arrested and charged with treason. The fact that

Dickstein is Jewish and one of the creators of the House Committee of Un-American Activities, intended to investigate Fascist activities in the United States in the 1930s, only fans the flames of anti-Semitism.

On August 8, 1946, President Dewey makes a public address to the American people, asking for calm. He assures the public that he and his cabinet will weed out all traitors in the government and military. He announces that he has submitted to Congress a bill extending investigative the powers of the FBI. The Congress passes the bill, and Hoover and his FBI begin to hunt down all communists and fellow-travelers through the government and military. Hoover warns that there is evidence of a Jewish-Communist conspiracy. Jewish and leftist groups are outraged and refer to Dewey as an American Hitler, and Hoover as the American equivalent of Heinrich Himmler. The Republican Party wins 86 out of 96 seats in the Senate, and 401 seats in the House of Representatives.

# REBUILDING GERMANY

In May 1946 Hitler announces his plans for the rebuilding of Germany now that the war is over. Hitler takes the responsibility for economic production away from Speer, and places Speer in charge of the reconstruction of German cities. In the next five years, the German people perform a miracle. The massive Allied bombing of Germany devastated large section of Germany's largest cities. The damage was not as great as it might have been if the war with the Americans and the British had continued pasted June 1944. But large sections of Hamburg, Berlin and Cologne were flattened during the war. Hitler announced that the Anglo-American air forces actually did Germany a great favor by clearing the way for him to rebuild their cities as he saw fit. Great monuments were built, especially in Berlin. A massive capital building was the first completed in Berlin. The dome was seven times bigger than the dome of Saint Peters in the Vatican. A huge arch of triumph was also built that dwarfed Napoleon's arch in Paris. In Hamburg, skyscrapers were built to rival those in New York City. Munich was refashioned as a cultural center. Hitler also ordered the massive reconstruction of his hometown, Linz, on the Danube River.

By 1951 Germany had repaired the damage inflicted upon it during the war. A vast autobahn network was built that stretch east to the Volga River. A new railroad system was also begun. The oilfields of the Caucasus and the Middle East were once again working at full capacity. Jet technology was underway and new plane designs were developed. Speer convinced Hitler that a series of huge airports should be planned and built throughout German dominated Europe. Speer also convinces Hitler that a passenger jetplane should be developed. The task was turned over to Messerschmidt, Heinkel and Junker companies. They set about competing among themselves to see who could build the best design.

# THE NEW ORDER IN EUROPE

November 9, 1946 Hitler calls a conference for all European states to meet in Berlin to form a new political, military and economic system. The New European Order is set up on January 1, 1947. The Greater German Reich is the dominate force in the alliance. Besides Germany, France, Spain, Portugal, Italy, Croatia, Slovakia, Romania, Hungary, Serbia, Greece, Bulgaria, Finland, Sweden, Britain, Ireland, the Caucasian Confederation and Russian Free State. All economic activities are coordinated from Berlin. Trade zones are set up that make Europe a centralized market. All military forces are under the command of the German General Staff.

Each nation retained control of their individual colonial empires. The African colonies belonging to the members of the New European Order are organized into a joint market system for the economic exploitation and colonization by the new Europe. All natives of Africa, with the exception of Egypt are reduced to slave labor. The former German colonies in Africa are returned to Germany plus the Belgian Congo and the French Congo. South Africa is granted full independence and is assigned a special allied-status with the New European Order. The Afrikaners are fully in control of South Africa. In the Middle East Egypt, Turkey, Iraq, Palestine, Saudi Arabia and Iran are all members of the Middle Eastern Alliance, which is allied to the New European Order.

In January 1947 SS Einsatzgruppen are sent to India to crush the growing Indian independence movement. Mohandas Gandhi is arrested and killed, while his Congress party is disbanded and its leaders are executed. Over two million people are killed by the SS in six months of fighting in India. A joint Anglo-German government is set up with the British in charge. Hitler has no desire to rule India, but does not want to see the British lose control.

On March 13, 1947, Switzerland is partitioned and the German populated region is annexed by Germany. Switzerland was a hotbed of espionage during the war. After the war many Communists and Soviet spies took refuge in Switzerland. The situation was intolerable for Germany. Leaders of Switzerland met with German leaders and arranged for the annexation of Switzerland. The Germans agreed that the Switz banks can continue to operate with a special arrangement. The SS immediately begins rounding up all Communists. Himmler discovers a communist ring that was in communication with Martin Borman. Borman was sending Germany most important military secrets to the Soviet Union. Borman is arrested. Hitler is devastated by the treason of one of his closest lieutenants. Goebbels, Goering and Himmler are all pleased. There is a purge of the district leaders of the NSDAP (National Socialist German Workers' Party). The power of the SS increases and the Party machinery loses influence.

# THE WESTERN HEMISPHERE ALLIANCE TREATY

On June 10, 1946, the Western Hemisphere Alliance Treaty (WHAT) is signed in Washington. It is an alliance that includes the United States, Canada, Mexico, Nicaragua, Guatemala, Honduras, Costa Rica, Panama, Columbia, Venezuela, Brazil, Ecuador, Peru, Chile, Paraguay, Uruguay, Paraguay, Bolivia, Haiti, the Dominican Republic, Cuba, Australia, and New Zealand. The Fascist Peron government of Argentina refuses to sign and allies itself with Germany and her allies. President Dewey meets with von Ribbentrop on July 16, 1946 and the two agree to recognize each other's spheres of influence. The United States agrees to respect the sovereignty of British, French, Dutch and Danish territories in the Western Hemisphere. In return Germany agrees not to interfere in the internal affairs of any of the signatories of WHAT.

President Dewey announces the need for a standing army and signs the Peacetime Selective Service Act on August 1. This is followed by the Armed Forces Bill on August 11. The laws provide for an army of one million men, and a two-ocean fleet. They also allow the development of jet and rocket technology.

On July 4, 1946, American occupation of the Philippines comes to an end. The Philippines are granted its independence and elections are held. The Philippines join WHAT.

On July 15, 1946, Prime Minister King of Canada announces that Canada will no longer a member of the British Commonwealth. Rejecting its status as a member of the British Commonwealth, a new constitution is drawn up and establishes a Canadian Republic. The new constitution creates a federal system with a president and congress similar to the government of the United States. But no sooner is the constitution adopted and elections held that trouble develops among the French-speaking province of Quebec. French-Canadians begin demanding independence for Quebec. The Free Quebec Party is the majority party in Quebec. Its leaders claim that since Canada is no longer part of the British Commonwealth, Quebec no longer recognizes itself as part of Canada. In the next six months violence escalates in Quebec and the Quebec Liberation Army begins a terrorist campaign. Canada is on the verge of civil war. President King requests the United States to send troops to prevent fighting between French and English-speaking Canadians. President Dewey agrees and American troops occupy Canada. A U.S.-Canadian commission is set up and new elections are held in February 1947. Quebec votes for independence while all English-speaking provinces vote by various majorities to seek admittance to the United States as states.

In February 1947, the newly elected Senator Joseph McCarthy heads up the House Committee on Un-American Activities and begins investigating Communist activities in America. J. Edger Hoover provides information that the film industry is riddled with communists. Anticommunist and anti-Semitic anger is directed against the major film companies, as well as against the news media and broadcasting corporations. Senator Lindbergh warns against "Jewish and communist sympathizers who would undermine the racial, cultural and political integrity of American civilization."

July 14, 1947 is declared Quebec Independence Day and Quebec is admitted to WHAT. By December 1947 the last of the Canadian provinces are admitted to the United States. Ten new states (British Columbia, Alberta, Saskatchewan, Manitoba, Ontario, Nova Scotia, New Brunswick, Prince Edward Island, Newfoundland and Labrador) are added to the United States, and the new fifty-eight-stars flag of the United States is unfolded for the first time.

On September 12, 1947, the U.S. Congress passes the Anti-Communist Bill that makes all Marxist, Communist, Socialist parties and organizations illegal. There is protest by the Left on how these terms will be defined. The American labor movement is split. Some of the larger Unions like the Teamsters declare that they are patriotic and anticommunist while the CIO and AFL attack the bill as unconstitutional. President Dewey is reluctant to sign the bill but finally does. Dewey was beginning to fear that America was slipping toward totalitarianism. His Secretary of State, Dulles leads the pro-German faction within the President's cabinet. He is supported by Charles Lindbergh, Joe McCarthy, and Robert A. Taft in the Senate as well as Joe Kennedy who is thinking of running for President. Southerners led by Governor Strom Thurmond of South Carolina, who support the racial laws of National Socialist Germany also support a pro-German policy. There is talk within the Republican Party of supporting a Lindbergh-Kennedy ticket for President in 1948. Opposition to this pro-German faction is led by the Rockefellers and Governor Earl Warren of California.

# CIVIL WAR IN CHINA

In June 1946 the Chinese Nationalists attack the Communists led by Moa Zedong. The Communists dominate Manchuria and parts of northern China. With American aid and support now arriving from Germany, the Nationalist offensive is successful. General MacArthur in Japan calls for additional support for the Nationalists. He even suggests that American troops in Korea should attack the Communist in Manchuria. Field Marshal von Manstein arrives in China as an advisor to the Nationalist army. Chiang Kai-shek is pleased with the assistance he receives from Germany and develops a friendship with von Manstein. MacArthur accuses President Dewey of "losing" China to Germany.

The Chinese Communists flee across the border into Siberia and Mongolia in July 1947. Zhukov, now President of Russia, meets with President Chiang of China and agrees to work together against Communism. President Zhukov announces that he will cut off the ugly head of Communism that caused the destruction of Mother Russia. The Russian-Siberian Federation attacks the Communists in Siberia, while Chinese troops invade and occupy Mongolia.

On September 3 Chiang declares the creation of Greater China and the restoration of a new Imperial Chinese Dominion. On September 14 Chinese troops and SS Einsatzgruppen invade Indo-China where the French are fighting the Vietnamese Communists.

# TECHNOLOGICAL ADVANCEMENTS

By July 1946 the United States begins production of its first jet fighter. By February 1947 the United States has its first long-ranger jet bomber. In October 1947 the Americans have developed a rocket equal to the German V-2. But the Americans are still far behind the Germans in jet technology.

The Germans have developed its A-15 three-stage rocket in August 1947. It can travel 12,000 miles and pass out of the atmosphere. After Germany returns to peace, the German rocket program eventually fall under the control of the SS. Werner von Braun meets with Himmler in November 1947. At the meeting, he makes a pitch for the further development of rocket technology. He first explaines the military applications of developing rockets that can strike a target anywhere on the planet, especially when armed with an atomic warhead. He then begins talking about sending a rocket into space and his dream of someday sending a man to the Moon and even to Mars. Himmler sits through the four-hour presentation without saying a word. Himmler gets up and looks at von Braun and says he would speak to the Fuehrer about his plans. Before he left, he asks von Braun how long it would take to put a man on the Moon. Von Braun said he could do it by 1957.

In November 1947 the Germans detonate their first atomic bomb north of the Caspian Sea.

By Jan. 1948 over one million Volkswagens are produced in Germany. Hitler hopes that in five years German production of automobiles will outpace American production.

In April 1948 German television goes into full production. German television is controlled by the government as is radio. Television becomes very popular in Europe. Goebbels sees the propaganda possibilities of television and wants every German family to have one by 1950. Hitler agrees and Speer is put in charge of the development of an inexpensive television set that everyone could afford.

# AMERICAN ELECTIONS OF 1948

In June 1948 the Democratic Party nominates Adlai Stevenson on the 51 ballot. Stevenson promises to fight racism and fascism in American and throughout the world.

Henry Wallace leaves the Democratic Party to run for president on the Progressive Party ticket.

In July 1948 the Republicans re-nominate President Dewey on the third ballot after agreeing to chose Lindbergh as his new vice presidential running mate. He was challenged by Senators Lindbergh and Vandenberg for the nomination. Dewey promises to continue to keep America strong and seek peaceful coexistence with Germany.

In November 1948, Dewey wins reelection as President, and receives 30,100,000 votes; Stevenson wins 9,500,000 votes; Wallace receives 600,000 votes. The Republican Party also retains control over both houses of Congress with over three-quarters of the seats.

In April 1949 President Dewey and Vice President Lindbergh are both in Berlin with leaders from Europe, South America, the Middle East and Asia for the celebration of Hitler's 60th birthday. Prime Minister Oswald Mosley of Britain is also there, as well as Mussolini from Italy, Franco from Spain, Chiang Kai-shek from China, Khuzov from Russia, Juan and Eva Peron from Argentina. Hitler addresses 100,000 people in the new Capitol Building. He announces that the name of the city of Berlin has been changed to Germania. Hitler also announces that the last of the Jews have been resettled on reservation in European Russia and Europe has been made Jew-free. President Dewey talks about greater economic cooperation between the United States and Germany. Powerful economic interests in the United States, led by the Rockefellers, seek to open European markets, Africa and western Asia that makes up the New Order.

On May 17, after President Dewey returns from Germania (Berlin) he is assassinated by Jewish terrorists. They claim their families were killed by the Nazis in Eastern Europe and that Dewey is another Hitler. Charles Lindbergh is sworn in as President and promises to weed out all anti-American elements within America. Joseph Kennedy is named Vice President. General MacArthur is called back from Japan and becomes head of a new American General Staff.

A new Japanese government is formed in June 1949. The Emperor is replaced with a republic similar to the United States, with a President, Congress and Supreme Court. Japan joins WHAT.

A Korean government is also formed in August 1949. It too is modeled after the United States' government and Korea joins WHAT.

In June 1949 Hoover is order by President Lindbergh to have the FBI begin a massive round up of Communists and other leftists throughout the United States. Senator McCarthy begins a Senate investigation of Communist and Jewish organizations in Hollywood. He claims that Hollywood is under Jewish-Communist control and seeks to destroy America. The House Committee of Un-American Activities amasses a list of over a million names of suspected Communists. Henry Wallace is arrested for treason. All Communist and Socialist organizations are arrested. Several powerful Jewish groups, including the Anti-Defamation League are also arrested. Over 500,000 people are arrested in the next year.

In July 1949, several pro-German organizations, Southern organizations, including the Klan, and pro-American organizations form the American Liberty Alliance. The ALA is backed by several large corporations who founded the American Liberty league in the mid-thirties to oppose Franklin D. Roosevelt.

In September 1949 the Twenty-Second Amendment to the Constitution is passed. It states that only Non-Jewish individuals of European descent (known as Aryans) can be citizens of the United States. It also states that only citizens of the United States are protected by the United States Constitution and U.S. laws.

In December 1949, President Lindbergh announces the formation of American Space Agency and declares that the United States will strive to put a man on the Moon. A space race with Germany begins.

# THE NEW GOVERNMENT OF THE GREATER GERMAN REICH

On January 30, 1950, the anniversary of Adolf Hitler ascension to power, Hitler announces the creation of a new constitution for the Greater German Reich. It will take three years for the constitution to become fully functional. A huge celebration was planned for the new constitution that will coincide with the twentieth anniversary of Hitler's rise to power. Hitler will become the President and a Chancellor will be appointed. The President will have great powers and his Chancellor will be his vehicle to carry out his policies, much like the American Secretary of State. A Senate will be formed. Senators will be chosen by the President and serve for life. A Reichstag will be created and its members will be elected by popular vote, and they will represent their individual districts. Future candidates for the Presidency will be chosen from the Senate and must receive a majority vote in the Reichstag, while the Chancellor must be a member of the Reichstag. Presidents will serve seven year terms.

Hitler also announces a massive program of colonization of European Russia by Germany. Settlers from all across Germany and the rest of Europe are encouraged to settle in communities that will be created by the government. Hitler is even hopeful that German-Americans will immigrate to the new territories in Eastern Europe. A certain number of Slavs are encouraged to accept Germanization along with all immigrants from the rest of Europe. Because of role that Russians played in the eventual defeat of the Soviet Union after Germany made peace with the Western Allies in 1944, the racial policies of Hitler and Himmler are modified. A greater percentage of Slavs are chosen for Germanization and the remainder of the Slavs of Russia are organized into self-governing ethnic districts that are allied to Germany. Forty percent of all Poles are encouraged to accept Germanization and permitted to remain in those sections of Poland that are annexed by Germany. The remainder of the Polish population is gradually relocated to communities throughout European Russia. They are mixed into a diverse population to prevent the formation of local Polish communities and in this way, the authorities hope they will be assimilated. Throughout the Eastern territories a Feudalistic hierarchy is created with the SS occupying the highest level. Below them are the general German population, followed by those Europeans who are undergoing Germanization. Next are the general European populations, and lastly those elements designated unsuitable for assimilation.

On March 23, 1950, Himmler announces the formation of the SS Foreign Legion. It incorporates the French Foreign Legion and the former overseas armies of the Belgians, the Portugese, the Spanish, the Italians, the Dutch and the British to form a mobile Army designed to maintain peace and order in European colonies throughout Africa and Asia. South African units are formed as well as an Egyptian unit.

Europe experiences a population explosion. Birth rates increase rapidly. Plans are made for additional settlements in Algeria, Tunisia, Libya, Kenya, Southern and Northern Rhodesia, and Italian East Africa. The native populations of Africa, India and the Middle East are stabile and even declining. In large sections of Africa the native black population is systematically being reduced.

By the end of 1950 there are less than four million Jews left in European Russia. The concentration camps of the war were dismantled and all Jews were resettled in the East, where they were used as slave labor under the most brutal conditions.

On April 30, 1950, the first man is sent into space by the Greater German Reich. Colonel Erich A. Hartman is sent into space in a new-class Donner Rocket launched from Peenemuende.

# CHINESE EXPANSION IN ASIA

By 1950 the Chinese Communists are eventually driven from Siberia and Mongolia by combined Chinese and Russian cooperation. Mao is killed in Siberia on September 21, 1950. The Communists are now led by Chou En-lai. He decides that the only hope for survival is to flee west. During the winter of 1950-51 he leads what's left of the Communist Army across Mongolia to Tien Shan and eventually into the former Soviet central Asian republics. By August 1951 the Communists recruit former Communists in central Asia and operate as bandits in the mountains of Kyrgyzstan.

President Chiang of China sends an army into western China in the summer of 1951. He occupies Tibet and meets with the Dali Lama, and promises to respect the autonomy of Tibet. The Nationalist Army of China begins operations in eastern Kazakstan, Kyrgyzstan and Tajikistan.

In Indo-China, the Communists operating there are eventually eliminated by the French Army supported by SS Einsatzgruppen and Chinese forces.

# UNITED STATES ELECTIONS

In March 1952 the United States passes the Twenty-Third Amendment to the Constitution. It sets guidelines for a Eugenics program similar to National Socialist Germany. Massive sterilization is planned for the black population. All citizens must carry a racial classification card. Plan Parenthood is made into a government agency. Its founder, Margaret Sanger, called for the sterilization of all nonwhites and the mentally incompetent. She also encouraged the best physical and mental individuals to produce large families. Many Christian groups oppose many of these programs, but Southern Christian groups support the white supremacy nature of the Eugenics programs.

Throughout the summer of 1952 White Racialist groups conduct acts of terrorism against blacks and Jews in the United States. Many Jews begin immigrating from the United States to Mexico and other Latin American Countries. The elections of 1952 are violent. Whites riot in many cities including New York City, Chicago, Los Angles and Detroit.

President Lindbergh and Vice President Kennedy are reelected by a landside in November 1952. The Democratic Party only received 20 percent of the vote.

# THE ARYANIZATION OF CHRISTIANITY

In February 1952 a continental meeting of European Protestant churches met in Germania. After one week the Protestant groups declare the formation of the United Church of Europe. It claims that only Aryans are true humans and possess a human soul. It also declares Jesus Christ an Aryan warrior who opposed international Jewry.

On May 1 1952 a meeting of Protestant groups convene in Atlanta. The majority of the churches presented sign a doctrine declaring only Aryans being fully human and possessing a human soul. They declare their solidarity with the United Church of Europe.

In September 1952 Pope Pius XII announces that the Catholic Church is in agreement with the decision with the United Church of Europe. Talks are conducted for the re-unification of Christianity.

## THE NEW GERMANY

January 30 1953. Adolf Hitler is sworn in as President of the Greater German Reich. Joseph Goebbels is appointed Chancellor. The majority of the new Senate is made up of SS members.

On April 10 1953, Adolf Hitler travels to the United States and meets with President Lindbergh in Washington. Hitler speaks before a joint secession of Congress and announces the signing of a new alliance between the New European Order and the Western Hemisphere Alliance Treaty. He declares a New Age for Aryan man has begun. Germany and the United States agree to combine their space program. Both the United States and Germany were working on the H-Bomb. It is agreed that both countries would form a joint agency to control the development of this new weapon. Both governments agree to work for closer integration over the next twenty years and the creation of a union of the NEO and WHAT, to ensure the domination of the Aryan Race throughout the world.

By 1953 most South American countries have Fascist governments in place, though they are still closer to the United States than to Germany. July 4 1957. A team of three Germans, two Americans and one Italian land on the Moon. Werner von Braun lives to see his dream of landing a man on the Moon fulfilled. He now announces that the nest step was to land a man on the planet Mars by 1970. President Lindbergh is reelected President in 1956. In Germany, Adolf Hitler does not accept renomination for President in 1960. He is seventy-one years old and very ill. He announces his retirement.

November 9, 1962, Adolf Hitler dies. World leaders from every country in the world attend his state funeral. President Joseph Kennedy Jr. from the United States is present, so is President Franco of Spain, President Peron of Argentina, President Romano Mussolini from Italy, President Chiang Kai-shek, King Edward VIII from Britain, who was restored to monarchy by the Germans, and many others. Hitler is temporarily enshrined in the great domed Capitol building and later his ashes are laid to rest is a tomb of his own design in his home town of Linz. President Speer, in his eulogy noted, "It was here, as a young man that Adolf Hitler first experienced a vision of his destiny. It was in these hills that Fate called a son of Germany to step forward and save Germany from the ashes of defeat and national humiliation and build a new Germany that stands as a light for the entire Aryan Race. Because of his unshakable faith in the German People, Aryan man now is the dominate force throughout the world and has taken the first steps on a new and glorious trek to the very stars themselves."

# WHAT IF THE GERMANS HAD ATTACKED MOSCOW IN 1942?

## BY
## ROBERT BLUMETTI

After the Soviet winter offensive of 1941-42 slowed to a halt, the German generals began to make plans to resume their own offensive in the Spring of 1942. The Germans are closing in on to Moscow, at some points, they are but one hundred miles away, Hitler refused to veto any plans to resume the attack against the Soviet capital. During the winter-spring months of 1942, the Soviets build up a formidable defense system between the German central front and Moscow. Numerous divisions are relocated between the Germans and Moscow, including the bulk of Soviet armor divisions and artillery. Stalin was determined to hold Moscow at all cost. But Hitler is interested in the oil fields in the Caucasus, and is not interested in destroying the bulk of Soviet forces. The German generals know this is a recipe for disaster and make contingency plans in case the opportunity arises. They continue trying to change Hitler's mind, but meet with little success. Hitler orders the OKW (command of the armed forces) to draw up plans for Operation Blue, the invasion of the Caucasus. The date is set for June 28.

# A CHANGE OF PLANS

At this point in time something happens to change the course of history. On May 2, a German general is flying near to the Soviet front when his air craft crashes. He is carrying the plans for Operation Blue. The plans fall into Soviet hands. (This actually happens in our time line, but it happens on June 19) When Hitler hears of the crash he flies into a rage. His generals convince him that the Soviets have plenty of time to prepare for their attack. They argue that the Soviets will avoid the German pincer movements by simply withdrawing across the Don River. If they are unable to encircle the bulk of Soviet forces at the outset of the offensive, Operation Blue will fail. The generals were convinced that the geographic reality dictated two choices for a possible offensive in 1942: at the central part of the front with Moscow as its objective or in the south with the Donets and the Caucasus as the objectives. Since the latter was now compromised, the Moscow offensive was the only logical choice. The capital was the central point of all Russian life. It is also the Western terminus of the land bridge between European and Asiatic Russia. After several days of considering his options, Hitler reluctantly agrees to call off Operation Blue. The OKW presents Hitler with a new proposal to begin in one week.

First, the 6$^{th}$ Army and the 1$^{st}$ Panzer army will cut off the Soviet forces in the Losovaya salient south of Kharkov. Once the southern front is fortified, the 11$^{th}$ Army under Manstein will be transferred to Leningrad and join the 18$^{th}$ Army in an assault on the besieged Soviet city. This assault will also eliminate the Oranienbaum bridgehead west of Leningrad, and destroy the Soviet salient around Yeglino, south of the city. This operation will begin on May 19. But the main operations will commence on June 28 along the central section of the front.

The German 16$^{th}$ and 9$^{th}$ armies will attack the Sukhinichi salient from the northwest while the 1$^{st}$ Panzer Army, to be transferred from the south, will strike north from Rzhev and entrap seven Soviet armies. The 2$^{nd}$ Panzer Army will attack north of Kaluga while the 4$^{th}$ Panzer Army will attack north from Orel and entrap another seven Soviet armies. Once these double entrapment maneuvers have been accomplished, the German forces, reinforced by Manstein's assault troops of the 11$^{th}$ Army, will attack Moscow in a great pincer movement. Hitler referred to this as Operation Red. Hitler agreed to this plan, but insisted that the 11$^{th}$ Army be transferred to the Crimea as soon as Moscow falls. He wanted to clear the Soviet forces held up in Sevastopol.

The OKW is convinced that the nature of these limited offensives will inflict heavy losses on the Soviets. It will also shorten the German lines and free existing forces, including the 18th Army and Finnish forces besieging Leningrad. By eliminating these pockets of resistance, at least three armies, including armored forces, could be freed in the sectors of Groups North and central. The German generals hope that the fall of Moscow will ne more than just a decisive military victors. They also believe it will both be a political and moral victory that will vastly weaken the Soviet Union. The Soviets have placed the bulk of their best forces defending Moscow. If Operation Red succeeds it will deal a massive blow to the Red Army, greatly disrupting Soviet operations. Moscow is an important center of traffic and arms production. The fall of the Red capital would mean the disruption of transportation and supply.

# THE OPPOSING SIDES

The German army was not fully recovered from the losses it suffered in 1941. By May 1942, it was only at two-thirds of its original strength when it invaded the Soviet Union in June 1941. Reinforcements have helped to replenish most of the German forces. In addition, fifty-four allied divisions were added from Germany's Slovakian, Romanian, Hungarian, Italian, Spanish and other allies. This did not include the fifteen Finnish divisions in the north. The Soviet army suffered a terrible beating and was no where as strong as it would be during the battle of Kursk in our time line. The German Army possessed a superiority of four-to-one over the Soviets in its quality of fighting abilities.

The Soviets were able to draw on its vast superiority in manpower, but its troops were poorly trained and not as well armed as they would be in 1943. In our time line, the Soviets' production of tanks and artillery will grow rapidly in 1942, because Moscow and the Russian heartland will not be overrun by the German army. This heartland, which is west of the Volga River, contains vast industries and manpower that would tremendously hurt the Soviet war effort if lost to the Germans. The Soviet Union in 1941 possessed four-major industrial centers: the Moscow region, the Donets Basin, the Urals and the Kuznets Basin in Western Siberia. The Germans partially captured the Donets Basin and almost captured Moscow. As a result, Soviet production actually declined by approximately 40 percent in 1941-1942. This decline was also compounded when the Soviets began dismantling and relocation of much of the Soviet industries and reassembled in farther to the east. It would not be until 1943 when Soviet production finally returned to its former 1940 strength. Still, the Soviets were able to field a much larger army than the Germans.

The German and Axis satellite troops in the Soviet Union in June 1942, totaled about 3.5 million. This figure includes 330,000 Romanians, 300,000 Finns, 70,000 Hungarians, 68,000 Italians, 28,000 Slovakians, 14,000 Spaniards, along with various other ethnic groups and nationalities fighting on the side of the Germans. The Soviets were able to field a much larger army. Soviet forces at the front was about 5.5 million troops, plus another 1.5 million in uncommitted reserve formations farther to the east. But despite these numbers, the Soviets were still far weaker than they were in June 1941. The Soviets could field 6,000 tanks to the Germans' 3,000 tanks. The Soviets had 2,600 combat aircraft while the Germans had 2,770. The Soviets possessed a superiority in artillery pieces, 55,000, while the Germans had only a fraction of this number, at 8,000. Further, the Germans lacked about 35,000 trucks and other motor vehicles. But numbers of men and equipment alone did not tell the whole story. The German combat effectiveness was far better than the Soviets and varied somewhere between ratios of 3.10 and 2.34 to 1. The qualitative factors were in the Germans' favor, for the Soviets still had not learned to fight as effectively as the Germans.

# MAY-JUNE 1942

The Germans began their offensive in early May. General Meckenberg led an attack on the Kharkov Salient with the 1$^{st}$ Panzer and 2 Army. The Soviets were butchered losing over 330,000 men. Simultaneously, Manstein began his offensive against Leningrad itself. The 16 Army struck at the Soviet salient north of Lake Ilmen, causing 100,000 Soviet losses. Further to the north the 3$^{rd}$ Panzer Army struck northeast, while the 18$^{th}$ Army attacked the Soviet 1$^{st}$ Army in the Oranienbaum pocket to the west of Leningrad. Manstein himself led the assault on Leningrad with the 11$^{th}$ Army. A concentration of the Luftwaffe on the city assisted the assault. The fighting was fierce and lasted for six weeks. In the end, the Germans succeeded in destroying the Oranienbaum pocket and smashed its way into Leningrad. The fighting was terrible, but the Soviets eventually surrendered. This happened after the Finns opened a second assault from the north. The Finns told the Germans they would not attack until the Germans linked with them east of Lake Ladoga. The German 3$^{rd}$ Panzer Army was able to reach the Finns on June 2. The Finns attacked Leningrad on June 6. The bridge line across Ladoga Lake was finally cut by the Germans on June 13, and Leningrad was finally isolated. The Soviet losses were about 1.3 million.

The Germans hoped to attack the Soviets on June 19, but delayed the attack until June 28 to permit the relocation of the 3$^{rd}$ and 1$^{st}$ Panzer Armies to the Central Front. With the capture of Leningrad, the Germans could now transfer both the 11$^{th}$ and 16$^{th}$ Armies to support the attack against Moscow, as well as free several panzer and infantry divisions for the North Africa theater. Meanwhile, the Germans were eliminating the Soviet pocket south of Rzhev. This had to be done before the assault on Moscow could begin. Over 100,000 Soviet losses were bagged in the Rzhev pocket. By the time the German offensive was to begin on Moscow on June 28, the Soviet losses for May-June 1942 were 1.7 million.

The main attack began on June 28. The German 3$^{rd}$ Panzer Army struck east from Demjansk and moved north of Ostaschhikov. Further to the north the 16$^{th}$ Army attacked across the Volkhov River. The German 1$^{st}$ Panzer Army struck north from Rzhev and linked up with the 3$^{rd}$ Panzer Army, encircling seven Soviet armies in the Toropec Pocket. A second German assault began with the attack of the 2$^{nd}$ Panzer Army toward Moschajsk and then moved south. North of Orel, the German 4$^{th}$ Panzer Army struck north, east of Kaluga. The two panzer armies finally met, resulting in the encirclement and destruction of eight Soviet armies. These two encircling movements resulted in the destruction of another 1.4 million Soviet troops. Stalin was determined to make a final last stand at Moscow. His refusal to permit a withdrawal ensured the encirclement of his armies by the Germans. The Red Army fought hard and the system of fortifications surrounding Moscow were well planned out. The Germans suffered heavy losses, but the fall of Leningrad freed the 16$^{th}$ and 18$^{th}$ Armies to support the German panzer thrusts. By ordering the red Army to resist fanatically, Stalin handed the Germans exactly what they were looking for: giant encirclement and pocket battles close to the Wehrmarcht's supply bases. This was the same kind of warfare the Germans had enjoyed the previous year before crossing the Dvina and Dnieper river lines.

After the completion of the double encirclement by August 1, the German armies now turned on Moscow. As in 1941, Stalin refused to abandon Moscow. Soviet reserves were rushed forward to meet the German panzer armies. But unlike 1941, this was August and the weather was warm and the ground was hard. There would be no rain or snow to plague the German armies as they resumed the attack on the Soviet capital. On August 5 the Germans resumed the attack with two great pincer movements north and south of Moscow. The 1$^{st}$ and 3$^{rd}$ Panzer Armies struck north of the city. The 3$^{rd}$ Panzer Army struck north of Kalinin while the 1$^{st}$ moved south and across the Moscow Canal. The 3rd Panzer was attacked by the Soviet 10$^{th}$ and 9$^{th}$ Reserve Armies, but was able to resume the attack after five days of heavy fighting. The 1st Panzer Army continued its progress slowly, blasting away through the heavy fortifications around Moscow with the support of the 9th Army. To the north the 16th Army was racing toward Rybinsk Reservoir.

Further to the south the German 2nd and 4th Panzer Armies attacked on both sides of Tula, encircling the city, continuing their assault east of Moscow. The two panzer armies suffered heavy losses, but they were able to fight off the attacks of the Soviet 70th and 6th Reserve Armies. After Rajasan fell to the Germans on August 25, the two panzer armies then turned north and linking up with the 3rd and 1st Panzer Armies at Vladimir on September 3. Moscow was now encircled and cut off from the rest of the Soviet Union.

# THE ENCIRCLEMENT OF MOSCOW

As the German armies moved to encircle Moscow, Stalin and the Soviet government fled to Gorki. As the Germans approached the Red Capital there was no replay of the civilian rebellion that took place the year before. The Soviet secret police, the NKVD, was out rounding up anyone who expressed any dissent. All civilians were rushed into service constructing defenses. Anyone who tried to escape the city was killed. The roads leading out of the capital were littered with the bodies of thousands of people who tried to flee. The Soviet defenses around Moscow were constructed in depth resembling a weaker version of the defense of Kursk in 1943, in out time line (OTL). Along the defenses the bulk of the Soviet reserve armies and newly reorganized tank corps were located.

Despite these defenses the concentrated German panzer thrusts penetrated into operational depths. The costs of these penetrations were high in men and equipment. But the Soviets refused to give ground. Even though Stalin fled, he left orders for every inch of ground to be defended to the last man. This permitted the bulk of the Soviet forces to be destroyed or encircled. Unlike OTL, when the Soviets withdrew across the Don River when the Germans attacked in the south, the Soviet armies were chewed up by German forces. Supported by both the 4th and 9th Armies that encircled Moscow, Manstein's 11th Army, experienced in assaulting fortifications, began the assault on the Red Capital. The fighting lasted for six weeks and the losses on both sides were terrible. As in out time line, when the Germans invaded the Caucasus, many Soviet citizens supported the Germans as liberators. In 1941 Hitler wanted to obliterate the entire city of Moscow and its civilian population, but this policy slowly changed with the defeats of the Winter 1941-42. After the Germans entered the Red Capital hundreds of thousands of Russians surrendered. Eventually, Manstein's 11th Army was able to pacify the city. When Moscow finally surrendered on October 1, the Soviets suffered another 1.3 million losses.

# THE RACE TO THE VOLGA

As Moscow was surrounded, the Germans tried to reach the Volga River before the rains of late October set in. The Germans took heavy losses, but they succeed in breaking through the Soviet lines and rapidly moved east of Moscow. The Soviet lines were ripped apart and the Red Army only put up token resistance. As the battle east of Moscow became more mobile, the Germans quickly achieved the advantage they needed. The Soviets' ability to fight a mobile battle had improved in the last twelve months, but the Germans were still superior when it came to mobile warfare. Now that the bulk of the Soviet forces on the Central front were destroyed or entrapped in Moscow, the Soviet front crumbled. Stalin was forced to flee once more to Kazan further east.

The German panzer armies continue to race eastward. Hitler soon grew nervous, but the German Generals convinced him that the Soviets could not put up any serious resistance east of the Volga. The 3rd Panzer Army reach Gorki while the 1st Panzer Army thrust toward Nizhiy Novgorod. The 2nd Panzer turned south and raced towards Penza while the 4th Panzer struck south to take Tambov. Further to the north, the German 16th and 18th Armies were pushing the Soviets back to a line from Lake Onego to Cherepovits.

As the Germans were pushing east on both the Central and Northern Fronts, the Soviets decided to conduct a massive withdrawal along the southern sector of the front. Front Voronezh to Rostov the Soviet armies began to withdraw east in a desperate attempt to block the Germans moving south toward the Don. The Soviets feared they would be entrapped on the west bank of the Don River by the Germans if they reached Stalingrad.

After the Soviet Union was not defeated, but their capacity to go on the offensive was servilely curtailed with the capture of Moscow and the destruction of the Soviet armies along the Central Front. This quickly led to the capture of the Russian heartland east to the Volga, resulting in the disruption of Soviet transportation and communication networks. But worst of all, the fall of the Russian heartland to the Germans meant the lost of one of the most important industrial centers and manpower reserve centers in the Soviet Union.

The Soviets were still able to crank out new equipment and train new troops, but only at the lower rates of 1941-1942. Only two major industrial centers were left to the Soviets, and Soviet production was reduced by 60 per cent. The lost of Moscow was also a major blow to Soviet morale. Revolts throughout the remainder of the Soviet Union were becoming more common. Stalin's own position as dictator was also in jeopardy. Revolts broke out among both anti-Communist forces and the many non-Russian nationalities. Stalin was faced with the fact that there would be no Soviet counteroffensive in 1942-1943. All Soviet reserves were being rushed to the front to set up fortifications along the Volga on a line that ran from Rostov to Stalingrad and up to Kazan.

# THE FAILURE OF OPERATION TORCH

After America entered the war, President Roosevelt wanted to concentrate the American war effort in Europe. With the Japanese overrunning most of the Pacific, FDR was desperate for an American victory somewhere. The American military wanted to land in France, but the British were completely opposed it. Churchill feared his government would collapse if an Anglo-American invasion of France failed. He still had nightmares about his failure at Gallipoli in the First World War. Churchill and Roosevelt settled on an Anglo-American invasion of French North Africa.

Roosevelt wanted the invasion to begin in October 1942, several weeks before the 1942 congressional elections. All polls indicated that the Democrats were going to do badly that November and could even lose control of the Congress to the Republicans. FDR hoped an American victory in North Africa could help the Democrats' chances at the polls in the elections. But the American military vetoed such a date as premature. The Allied forces would not be ready at such an early date and planned the invasion for November 8, after the elections.

With the defeats of the Soviet armies in the summer of 1942, and the encirclement of Moscow, Stalin became more desperate and began demanding the Western Allies do something to relieve the pressure on the Soviet Union. He wanted a second front established in France as soon as possible. FDR puts pressure on the military forcing them to move the date up to October 8. The result is a total disaster. When the Americans landed in North Africa, the French decided to resist due to of the exceptional German victories on the Russian Front. In September 1942 Hitler transferred several panzer and infantry divisions to North Africa to reinforce Rommel. Half of the force is moved into Algeria and Tunisia to support the French. The Americans are driven back into the sea and Vichy France officially joins the Axis against the Allies. The British land, unaware of the American defeat. By the time they learn of the American disaster they are attacked by the French with German support. The rest of the German reinforcements don't arrive in time to prevent a British victory at El Alamein, but Rommel is once again able to halt the British advance in Libya at El Agheila. Rommel stops Montgomery once again and turns the tide on December 16. The reaction to the disaster in North Africa, the Republicans take control of both houses of Congress.

1942 was a year of victories for Germany, but the German armies were exhausted. The cost of German victories on the Eastern Front resulted in the reduction of the strength of the German forces by one third. The Soviet armies were worst off, but the Soviets could raise new divisions at a faster rate, though it took time to train and equipment their new recruits. Stalin decided not to counterattack the Germans in 1942, but instead, to dig in and build up his forces for 1943. He still demanded that the Western Allies invade France, and was furious at the Anglo-American defeats in North Africa. He accused the Allies of not trying hard enough to defeat the Germans and began to seek the possibility of a separate peace with Germany.

Churchill and Roosevelt agreed to meet in Canada in February 1943. Roosevelt wants to push forward a Germany first strategy but he needs a victory somewhere in the Western theater. The defeat of the Japanese Navy at the Battle of Coral Sea and the Battle of Midway convinces the American military that the war should be concentrated on defeating Japan first. They are also convinced that the Anglo-American forces are not yet ready to take on the Germans. The Battle of the North Atlantic was still raging, and until the Allies could eliminate the threat of the German U-boats they would never be able to build up their forces for an assault on Europe or North Africa. Roosevelt is forced to agree and authorizes a major build up in the Pacific. Southern Democrats in both houses of Congress have joined with the Republicans to undermine Roosevelt's authority. They want a Japan First war strategy. Roosevelt fears that any further defeats in Europe would result in his defeat in the 1944 elections and surrenders to the pressure to concentrate in the Pacific. It is agreed that America's military efforts across the south and central Pacific will commence as soon as possible. Roosevelt also wants to increase lend-lease to the Soviets. He is bent on pleasing Stalin. To achieve this goal the United States would have to decrease the amount of aid to the British, which angers Churchill. Churchill fears Roosevelt and the Americans are too naive when it comes to Stalin and the Communists. To satisfy the British, Roosevelt also promises to send American infantry tank divisions to Egypt and the Middle East, to fight alongside the British.

# GERMAN PLANS FOR 1943

Hitler is delighted with the progression of the war, but he is concerned about the limited oil supplies available to his forces. He feared that his future offensives would be limited by his lack of oil to supply his forces. He wanted to pursue the Soviets south across the Don River and into the Caucasus but his armies ran out of fuel. He is desperate for the oil the Caucasus could provide and claims that if his generals had followed his plans for Operation Blue in 1942, Germany would now have all the oil she needed. Throughout the Winter and Spring of 1943 Stalin continues to seek out for a negotiated settlement with the Germans, but Hitler wants to capture the Caucasus before agreeing to a settlement with the Soviets. Plans are drawn up for a another offensive into the Caucasus in June 1943. Hitler finally agrees to place the German economy on a total war footing. Hitler also orders the manufacturing of the new Me 263 jet fighters.

Hitler agreed to the total mobilization of the Germany economy, which was accomplished by the end of January 1943. This benefitted German production and set manpower free for the Wehrmacht. Eight hundred thousand men were drafted during the first half of 1943, and the Hitler finally approves the draft of women for work in manufacturing plants.

Because of the defeat of the Anglo-American invasion of North Africa, the Italians don't overthrow Mussolini. At the same time Rommel is ordered to resume the offensive in Libya. He is instructed to attack the Allies in Egypt and invade the Middle East. With the entrance of Vichy France into the war, Rommel's rear is now protected. The Germans are able to use bases in Tunisia to supply Rommel. Rommel wants an assault on Malta before he resumes his attack against the British. Hitler agrees to an attack on Malta. The Germans hope to link up with their forces moving south through the Caucasus into Iran. Feelers are put out to Japan to resume the attack on India for a grand strategy of the Axis linking up in Iran. The Japanese are reluctant to commit their fleet to the Indian Ocean after their double defeat by the Americans at Midway and Coral Sea.

The Vichy government is reluctant to become involved in the war, but with the Germans in North Africa they have to submit to Hitler's demands. The Vichy French try to convince Hitler to release the two million French prisoners of war. Hitler agrees to release one million if they volunteer for duty in North Africa and in Russia. Half are sent to Russia and placed under German command. They take up defensive positions along the Volga. Several infantry divisions are placed under Rommel's command to fight against the British. Rommel is able to win over the loyalty of these French divisions as they prove to be courageous and dedicated soldiers fighting the British, who they hate.

## OPERATION OILFIELDS

On June 25, 1943, the German armies struck south into the Caucasus. The Germans were employing their new Tiger and Panther tanks. As the rushed forward, the Soviet armies began withdrawing. The Soviets were expecting the Germans to attack in the south and decided not to stand and fight as they did at Moscow. The Soviet armies had not yet recovered from their defeats in 1942. The Red Army had less territory to draw on and spent most of their resources building a series of fortifications on the east bank of the Volga. Even with the lost of the Russian heartland, the Soviets still had a great industrial capacity in Siberia and the Urals. The Soviets were able to build new armies with the support of American Lend-lease, but it would not be until late 1943 before they could buildup a sufficient reserve of their T-34 tanks for an offensive. By avoiding direct battles with the Germans, the Soviets can build up their armies and wait until the Germans are exhausted. As the German panzer armies are racing south, Stalin is planning a major offensive further north.

By October 1943, the Germans have reached the Caucasus Mountains and have reached the oil fields. The Caucasus peoples, especially the Cassocks, welcome the Germans as liberators. The Soviets blowup the oilfields as they retreat. For the next month the Germans sludge it out over the mountains, but they finally cross over to the south. Baku is captured on November 15. The Georgian and Armenian peoples also welcome the Germans as liberators.

## NORTH AFRICA AND THE MIDDLE EAST

In January 1943, a combined German-Italian-French assault on Malta begins. The overall importance of Malta's position in the Mediterranean for future Axis was emphasized by Rommel, Field Marshal Kesselring, the German Navy and the Italian Comando Supremo. They were able to convince Hitler of the great advantage that laid in Axis possession of the island. An air offensive began by the 2nd Air Corp. of the Luftwaffe on January 2 and the 28 with all its forces. The British suffered such heavy loses that it was paralyzed to resist an Axis invasion. The Luftwaffe flew 5800 bombers, 6000 fighter and 350 reconnaissance missions and deployed over three hundred aircraft in these operations. This was followed by an assault by the French and Italian fleets against the British defenses as German

Airborne troops take both airfields after heavy losses. This is followed up by a German-Italian assault by sea. After three weeks of heavy fighting and high casualties on both sides, Malta finally falls to the Axis. The Central Mediterranean is finally secured by the Axis.

Now that Rommel's supply lines are secured with the capture of Malta, he resumes the attack in Libya. This time he is reinforced by several Panzer divisions and additional French troops. Rommel defeated Montgomery at El Aghelia in March 1943, and again at Tobruk in May 1943. The British defeat was total. Montgomery was removed from his command in disgrace. In June 1943, Rommel once again crosses into Egypt. This time his Africa Corp. is met by a combined force of British and Americans. With the defeat of Operation Torch, the Allies began transferring the American 7th Army to Egypt. Since Montgomery was removed from his command, it was agreed that an American should be put in charge of the Anglo-American forces in Egypt. Churchill fears that Turkey will come into the war on the side of the Axis and agrees to the Americans' demand. The Allies pick General Patton. The Second battle of El Alamein is fought in October 1943. Both sides are evenly matched and the battle is fought to a standstill.

The Ally command wants Patton to retreat to Alexandria and wait for reinforcements, but Patton refuses. He figures that if his armies are in bad need of supplies, so are Rommel's armies. He decides to open a surprise attack in November 1943. His gamble pays off. Patton's attack takes Rommel by surprise. Once again both sides suffer terrible losses, but Rommel believes that the only way the Allies could resume the attack is because they have received reinforcements. Rommel has outrun his supply lines and his supplies haven't reached him yet. Fearing a total route by his badly under strength forces, he decides to play it safe and retreats to Tobruk. Patton receives his supplies and continues to attack. He doesn't want to give Rommel time to catch his breath.

# THE SOVIET WINTER OFFENSIVE OF 1943-44

In November 1943 the Soviets finally go on the offensive. In the Caucasus the Red Army retreated while they built up their forces along the Volga River. Soviet armies stationed on the north bank of the Volga between Gorki and Kazan attack to the south while another offensive was launched between Kazan and Saratov. The Germans are determinated, but they are unable to stop the Soviets. Their best forces, most of the panzer units were in the Caucasus. The Soviets were trying to recapture most of the Russian heartland between the Don and Volga Rivers. Hitler gave orders for his armies to hold their positions and fight for every inch of territory. Field Marshal Manstein was sent north to stop the Soviets. He was able to strike at the advance guard of the Soviet spearhead that had taken Voronezh. The German 3$^{rd}$ and 4$^{th}$ Panzer armies to the Central Front with their newest Panther and Tiger tanks. They counterattacked in February and encircled five Soviet armies at Voronezh, forcing the Soviets back to a line that ran from Rbinsk in the north to Vladimir, Ryazin, Tambov, along the Khoper and Don Rivers to Stalingrad.

# ALLIED NORTH AFRICAN OFFENSIVE OF 1944

Because of the Soviet offensives in the East, Hitler was unable to send additional reinforcements to Rommel in North Africa. Patton's armies were now at full strength once again and he resumed his attacks on Rommel. Patton attacks Rommel at Tobruk and breaks through the Axis lines in December 1943. Rommel is in retreat and withdraws to El Aghelia, but is unable to stop Patton. The Allied armies in North Africa are now receiving uninterrupted supplies and reinforcements. The Allies were able to turn the tide in the North Atlantic in 1943. Reinforcements and supplies were now crossing the Atlantic in record numbers. In February 1944, the British and American fleets sail into the Mediterranean attacking the French and Italian fleets, seriously destroying them. The Vichy governments in Algeria, Morocco and Tunisia are secretly opening up negotiations with the Americans.

Patton once again is able to force Rommel to retreat, this time to Tunisia. The Germans formally take over the administration of Tunisia. Patton's offensive has finally run out of steam, but in the west, American and British forces once again land in North Africa in April. This time the Vichy governments surrender to the Allies and Morocco and Algeria are quickly overrun. With the surrender of Vichy governments in North Africa, Hitler orders to total occupation of Vichy France. Surprisingly, those French troops under Rommel's commander agree to continue fighting for Rommel. The final battle for the North would now begin. Allied attacks from Libya and Algeria begin in May and last two months, when Rommel convinces Hitler to withdraw 300,000 German and Italian troops to Sicily for that island's defense. The German control of Malta prevents the Allies from invading Sicily.

# THE SOVIET SUMMER 1944 OFFENSIVE

Allied air raids against Germany increase and German cities now feel the weight of Allied bombardment. FDR wanted to invade France in 1944, but the invasion had to be postponed until 1945. Churchill wants to concentrate Allied operations in the Mediterranean. With the Caucasus in German hands most of the oil fields are reopened by the summer of 1944. Badly needed oil now flowing into the German economy. Hitler is determined to retain control of the Caucasus.

Stalin, on the other hand, is planning to take back the Caucasus during the summer of 1944. The Soviet economy's production is greater then Germany's at this junction but not by much. The lost of the Caucasus not only causes great hardships on Soviet production because of the lost of its oil reserves, but also eliminates the supply lines arriving from the United States. The lost of Moscow also meant the lost of the Soviets' vast rail network west of the Ural Mountains. This hampered the movement of both troops and supplies to the front. American army trucks were now more valuable then ever, but their numbers were limited by the poor roads and rail links through Central Asia, which was now the only means for supplying the Soviets year round.

In July 1944, the strength of the Red Army along the entire front with Germany was 6.4 million men, 8,200 tanks and self-propelled guns and 8,250 aircraft. The Soviets faced 3.9 million Axis troops, of which 900,000 were non-Germans, 380 tanks and self-propelled guns and 2700 aircraft. The Soviet Summer Offensive began on July 7 all along the front from Ryazan to the Don River. A second attack began five days later across the Volga between Stalingrad and Astrakhan. The Germans and their allies resisted courageously, but they were outnumbered and overwhelmed. The Germans were forced to withdraw and tried to set up a new line along the Don River, but the Soviet broke through this line as well. Voronezh fell to the Soviets, but the Germans were able to stop the Red Army from taking Kursk and Orel. Further to the south the Soviet overran Kharkov. On August 18 Rostov fell, cutting off the Caucasus from the Ukraine. The Germans in the Caucasus were forced to retreat south. Hitler refused orders to issue for their to withdrawal before they were cut off entirely. He wanted to retain control of the oil wells at all cost. In the South the Germans were able to establish a line at the Caucasus Mountains. Hitler hoped to transport oil across the Black Sea to Romania and the southern Ukrainian ports. The Germans under Manstein were able to launch a series of counterattacks and retook Kharkov pushing the Soviets back to Rostov, but failed to reestablish contact with the Caucasus.

# THE ALLIED INVASION OF GREECE AND SICILY

During the Summer of 1944 the Allies decided they would have to take Malta before they could invade either Italy for Greece. Churchill had pushed for invasions of southern Europe and still opposed a cross channel invasion of northern France. He feared a defeat in northern France could result in the collapse of his government, and the withdrawal of Britain from the war. Britain's economy was on the verge of collapse and was only kept afloat by large injections of aid from the United States. British manpower was also running out. He wanted to conduct smaller invasions of Italy and Greece to prevent further drains on British manpower. Churchill also hoped to prevent the Soviets from overrunning Eastern Europe. He wanted to restore British influence in the Balkans and Central Europe after the war.

In April 1944, a combined Anglo-American assault on Malta was successful. The Germans fought hard to retain the island, but the Allied navies now dominated the Mediterranean. The Island surrendered after three weeks of hard fighting. The fall of Malta was fallowed by the invasion of Crete in June. This time the Allies had to assault the island with 50,000 troops. Once again the Germans fought to defend every inch territory and the losses to both sides were heavy. After six weeks of fighting, Crete was finally in Allied hands. Hitler was forced to rush badly needed troops from the Russian Front to reinforce his defenses in both Italy and Greece.

On August 4, 50,000 Allied troops landed in Greece. Three amphibious assaults were launched. Athens and the Peloponnese fell to the Allies, but the Germans and Italians were able to establish a line of defense across the neck of the Boeotia. Greece proved to be a difficult terrain for the Allies to invade. The mountains of Greece provided a natural defense for the Germans to dig into. Despite Greek partisan activities to the rear of the Germans, the Axis were able to prevent the Allies from breaking out of southern Greece.

A second Allied amphibious invasion began in November against Sicily. The British land south of Siracusa, while the Americans under Patton land near Palermo. As the British moved north, along the eastern coast of the island, the Americans moved west on the northern coast. The battle was costly. There were over 400,000 German and Italian troops on the island and they fought fiercely to defend every inch of territory. The Italians fought harder in this time line than in our own because of the slower progression of the Anglo-American advance, the defeat of Torch in 1942, and the German successes in the Soviet Union in 1942 and 1943. But the Allies were able capture the entire island by November. This sent repercussions through the Fascist Italian government.

During this Roosevelt's health was getting progressively worst. The failure of Operation Torch, and the postponement of the invasion of France in 1944 caused FDR's health to deteriorated even more than in our time line. Roosevelt wanted to concentrate the American war effort in Europe, but the failure to do this aggravated his mental and physical condition accelerating his decline. By early 1944 he suffered several minor heart attacks and his physicians restricted him to a twenty-hour work week, but even this was too much for him. By March 1944, he had been reduced to a raving lunatic. Henry Wallace was unpopular with much of Roosevelt's cabinet and the running of the government suffered. Then, on May 5, Roosevelt died. Wallace was sworn in as the President of the United States. Eleanor Roosevelt encouraged Wallace to declare his intension to run for President in 1944. Wallace was able to retain the support of the New Dealers within the Democratic Party, but lost the support of the Southern Wing of the party. The Southerners walked out of the Democratic Convention in 1944 when Wallace received the nomination of the Democratic Party. The Southerners formed the States' Rights Party with Strom Thurmond, from South Carolina, as their candidate. The Republicans nominated Thomas E. Dewey from New York. Wallace proves to be too radical for the American people. With the Democratic split and demoralized, Thomas E. Dewy goes on to win the Presidency in November 1944.

# WAR IN THE PACIFIC, 1944

Following of the defeat of Operation Torch in 1942 and the fall of Moscow, the American Military convinces FDR to increase the forces allocated for the Pacific. It was agreed by both the British and American military leaders that any attempt to invade North Africa would have to be put off for a year, and an invasion of northern France for a further two years at least. American forces in the Pacific were now strengthened. With the defeat of the Japanese at Coral Sea and Midway, the Americans were now in position to begin rolling back the Japanese Empire. Throughout 1943, the American forces attack in the southern Pacific theater (invading New Guinea), and in the central Pacific (the invasion of the Gilbert Islands and Guam), and the Aleutian Islands were recaptured.

By 1944 the American Navy was now superior to the Japanese Navy everywhere in the Pacific. But the Japanese Navy was still a serious threat. The Americans continued to advance throughout 1944. Palau Island fell to the Americans in June, and the Philippines were invaded and liberated in August. The Mariana Islands fell to the Americans in March and Iwo Jima fell in May. A large naval battle was fought between the American and Japanese fleets at the Battle of the Lingayen Gulf in June, resulting in the complete destruction of the Japanese Navy. The Americans now ruled the Pacific. In September the island of Formosa was invaded. Formosa was considered Japanese home territory, and the American suffered heavy casualties. After six weeks of terrible fighting, the island was secured. The Americans quickly followed up their capture of Formosa with the invasion of Okinawa in December. Once again Japanese resistance was fanatical.

On the mainland of China the Japanese Army began to invade southern China. The Chinese Nationalist forces suffered heavy loses but refused to surrender. The Japanese were able to link up with their forces in southern China. To counter Japan's advance in southern China, the British began a counter attack in Burma. They hoped to open the Burma Road to China. This was achieved in early 1945 and badly needed supplies began to flow into China to support the badly mauled Nationalist forces.

# AIR WAR IN EUROPE 1944-45

Throughout the war the British had been escalating the air war against Germany. British policy was terror bombing. They believed that saturation bombing of residential neighborhoods was more effective than the destruction of factories, military and scientific facilities. But the British found it difficult to conduct raids on Germany without suffering heavy loses during daytime hours, and so they conducted their raids during at night. After the Americans entered the war, they preferred to conduct daytime bombing against strategic targets. Throughout 1943, round-the-clock bombing began to take its toll. The principal target was the vital industrial area of the Ruhr Valley, but it was not restricted to the Ruhr. Throughout Fortress Europe from Norway in the north to Italy in the south, the Allied bombers flew on their errands of death and annihilation.

German war production was heavily damaged by these raids, but it was by no means crippled. The war plants recovered quickly, some even increasing their output despite repeated raids. Efforts were made to continue war production in vast underground plants.

German production continued to increase. Production of aircraft by the Germans increased from 15,288 in 1942 to 25,094 in 1943, to 39,275 in 1944 and 47,833 in the first seven months of 1945. In this time line German production took a different turn because of the introduction of new German jet fighters and bombers. In this time line, the Germans had access to a larger supply of oil for a longer period of time. In our time line, the Germans produced hundreds of the Messerschmidtt Me 262 jet fighters, but very few got off the ground because of the fuel shortage. But in this time line that does not happen. By August 1944, hundreds of Me 262s were being produced every month were plenty of the fuel and trained pilots to fly them. This caused a reduction in the effectiveness of the Allied air raids on Germany in the second half of 1944 and throughout 1945. Soon after the Me 262 went into production, several other jet fighters were produced. The most effective fighter was the Heinkel He 162 Volksjaeger. It was a single engine design that was easy to manufacture. Heinkel was able to begin production of the Volksjaeger within six weeks after he completed its design. By May 1945, over one thousand were being produced in Germany's underground factories. It also proved very effective in challenging the Allies for dominion of the skies over Germany.

The Allies continued to inflict severe damage on Germany, but at a very high cost to themselves. The British would lose over 130,000 airmen and 47,000 planes by war's end. The Americans would suffer the lost of 48,000 planes and the death of over 111,000 airmen. In this time line the Allies were unable to continue their one thousand plane raids. The Allies were never able to conduct raids that produced the destruction that was inflicted on Dresden in out time line. The Germans made a massive effort to drive the Allies from the skies over Germany in early 1945. With the mass production of the Me 262 and the He 162, Allied loses of both fighters and bombers were as high as 30 to 40 percent throughout 1945. The cost in planes and manpower for the Allies began to skyrocket.

The Germans had also invented the V-1 rockets in 1944, and begun unleashing them against Britain in June. This was followed by the V-2 rockets in September. The V-2s traveled faster than the speed of sound. Though neither of these rockets were very effective, they had a terrible psychological effect on British morale. But was even more devastating was the introduction of the two-staged V-3, or "American Rocket" in June 1945. Hundreds of V-3s were launched from Germany and raced across the Atlantic. Most fell harmlessly into the Atlantic, but several dozen struck New York City, as well as New Jersey and New England. Worst still was the introduction of the Horton Flying Wing.

Goering had authorized the production of a flying wing designed, six-engine, long-range jet bomber designed by two brothers, Walter and Reimar Horten. The first flying wing jet bombers conducted a raid on New York City. Fifteen bombers took off from Germany on June 17 and flew at a height of 37,000 feet.

Several other raids would take place in July and August, as well as raids on Soviet cities in the Ural Mountains. The war suddenly came home to the Americans.

# SOVIET WINTER OFFENSIVE OF 1944-45

The year 1944 was one of Soviet advancement. The Soviet economy had finally reached a point where it was producing enough tanks, guns and plans to permit the Red Army to conduct a massive offensive. The Soviets shrewdly timed their attacks, working in close coordination, and maintaining their supply lines on the few railroads they still controlled, attacking westward through the Ukraine. The Red Army advanced 400,000 miles across the Dnieper River.

Fighting began on an 800-mile front in the south, running from Tula, south of Moscow to Orel, Kursk, Byelgorod to Kharkov and down to Rostov. A secondary attack took place in the north between Lake Onega and Cheropovets, advancing 100 miles, taking Byelozark, but failing to reach Lake Ladoga and Leningrad. The German 18th Army and their Finnish allies put up stiff resistance in the swamps and rough terrain of this northern region.

On November 3, the Soviets captured Kharkov and crossed the Donets River. On November 4 Kursk fell, followed by Orel on November 8. With the capture of these three key cities, the Germans found it difficult to maintain their line of defense. The Germans were forced to retreat, but before they did the Wehrmacht and the Luftwaffe systematically destroyed all three cities, leaving them in flames.

The impetus of the Soviet drive continued into December. The Soviets sought to retake Kiev, the capital of the Ukraine, and cross the Dnieper River to cut off the German forces in the Crimea. The Soviet Tide swept on irresistibly for the next two months. Key points fell to the Soviets, one after another. Dnepropetrosk, Zaporrozhye, Krivai Rog in the south and Gomel and Bryansk in the north. But the Soviets were finally halted before they could take Smolensk, and they failed to reach the mouth of the Dnieper River which would have cut off the Crimea.

When the Soviet offensive finally outran its supply lines, the Germans struck back on February 5, 1945. Using mobile maneuvers, the Germans were able to retake Krivai Rog in the south, pushing the Soviets back across the Dnieper River. North of Kiev the Germans retook Gomel and reached the outskirts of Bryansk. The Germans finally retook Kiev. Their Ukrainian allies fought along side the Germans, determined to liberate their capital.

Further to the south, in the Caucasus, the Soviets attacked across the Caucasus Mountains. The German 11th Army, which was sent there to storm the last

Soviet pockets of resistance in 1944, had been trapped there after the Soviet Summer 1944 offensive. Local populations had welcomed the Germans as liberators from Soviet Communism. Units of Georgians, Armenians, Azerbaijanis, Chechyans, Dagestanis and Cossacks all joined the Germans as allies in the hope of preventing the Soviets from retaking the Caucasus.

The British attacked from the south where they had occupied Iran since 1942. The British struck north and eventually took Baku, but not before the Germans destroyed all the oil wells there. The 11$^{th}$ Army under Field Marshal Busch retreated to the Turkish border. They fought their way south, putting up stiff resistance against the advancing Soviets. Native guerillas remained behind, in the mountains, and harassed the Soviets. Hitler had ordered Busch to fight to the end. He did not want to surrender the oil wells to the Soviets, but the Germans were not match for the Red Army. Hitler wanted to try to keep the 11$^{th}$ Army supplied through the Black Sea, but it was impossible. Hitler finally was able to put pressure on the Turkish government to agree to permit the 11$^{th}$ Army to retreat into Turkish territory, where it was eventually returned to Germany. The 11$^{th}$ Army suffered 50 percent casualties, but the Soviets lost over 800,000 casualties.

The first German jet fighters appeared on the Eastern Front during their counterattack. Me 262s were instrumental in halting the Soviet advance and driving them out of Kiev. In this time line the Soviet do not dominate the skies over the Eastern Front. Hundreds of Soviet tanks were destroyed by German jets. Shortly after the fall of Kiev to the Germans, the German jet bomber, the Arado 234 made its first appearance. It was an effective instrument in disrupting Soviet supply lines. The appearance of German jets had the effect of slowing the advance of the Soviet Army during 1945.

# THE FALL OF ITALY 1944

In this time line Mussolini is able to maintain control over his Fascist government until October 1944, when he is finally overthrown. The lost of Sicily and Italy's Italian empire had convinced the Italians that they had nothing to gain by staying in the war. General Badaglio and the Italian King negotiated secretly with the Allies to drop out of the war. When they thought they had assurances from the Allies that Italy would be permitted to surrender, the King arrests Mussolini and replaces him as Prime Minister with Badaglio.

Badaglio assures the Germans that Italy will remain loyal, but Hitler is not fooled. Before the Allies can invade Italy, the Germans invade, occupying the entire country down to the Italian toe. Hitler immediately reinstates Mussolini, but this time as head of state. The King and Badaglio flees the country and the Monarchy is replaced by the Italian Fascist Republic.

# THE INVASION OF FRANCE JUNE 1945

Churchill had been sending reinforcements to Greece for an attempt breakout into the Balkans in the Spring of 1945. The Germans were too preoccupied in Russia to release enough troops to drive the British back into the sea. Churchill still objected to an invasion of Northern France. He knew Britain was exhausted from five and a half years of war. He feared that the British Empire could not survive the type of losses it suffered in the war of attrition during the First World War. He preferred to fight Germany at the periphery of German-occupied Europe, far away from the center of German power.

The Americans were determined to invade France. The American Army in Europe now numbered over two million and President Dewey is anxious to land this army in France. Churchill had been dragging his feet for three years, but he knew that he could no longer delay a cross-channel invasion. Churchill agreed to only one British Army joining the invasion. The Americans would send four divisions across the channel to land in Normandy. The British could provide additional air and sea power to support the invasion, but Churchill wanted to concentrate British power in Greece. The Allies agreed that once they had established a beach head in Normandy, the British would break out of the Greek beach head. In this way they could apply pressure on the Germans from two directions. Churchill agreed to this plan. He was concern about the Soviets overrunning eastern and central Europe and hoped to drive north through the Balkans to prevent the Soviets from occupying Romania, Hungary, Yugoslavia and Bulgaria. Churchill believed this strategy would ensure the British Empire remained a great power in the postwar world. Having no illusions about Stalin, he was relieved when FDR died and Dewey became President replacing Henry Wallace. Both FDR and Wallace were too trusting of the Soviets. There were over 300 Soviet agents within the Roosevelt-Wallace administration, many in high positions responsible for the formulation of policy toward the Soviet Union. But Dewey was far less trusting of Stalin and was glad to cooperate with Churchill in planning the postwar settlement. Dewey even agreed with Churchill that FDR's "Unconditional Surrender" policy was a big mistake scrapping.

On June 4, four American and one British division landed on the beaches of Normandy. The weather was clear and perfect for the invasion. Several weeks before the invasion the Allies conducted massive carpet bombardment of northern France knocking out communication and transportation junctions, as well as smashing as much of the German fortifications along the coast. In this time line, Rommel was able to convince Hitler that he should order the positioning of the panzer armies close to the coast in 1945. When the Allies invaded Normandy in 1945, they were confronted with panzer assaults by King Tiger and Panther tanks. In addition to the panzer assaults, the Allies were confronted with swarms of German Jet fighters and bombers that challenged Allied air supremacy. The Americans and British were developing their own jet fighters, but they would not be ready for another month. Churchill tried to convince the Americans to postpone the invasion until after their jet fighters could become available to assists in the invasion. He feared the German jets would deny the Allies air superiority and put the entire operation in jeopardy. The Allies were able to hold onto their beach heads throughout June, but found it difficult to breakout from Normandy into France. Both side suffered heavy losses. By July 1, the Allies lost air superiority and the Germans were able to move their panzer reserves stationed in the Flanders to Normandy without fear of being destroyed by Allied air attacks. Churchill's prediction about the threat of German jets were coming true.

Despite the German attacks from their panzer armies and jets, the Allies were able to build up their armies strength on their beach heads. By July 14 they attacked the German lines, using their new jet fighters to challenge the German jets. The Americans were able to break out under Patton between Coutance and St. Lo and struck towards Rennes and e Mans. The Germans sent their panzer reserves to attack from Argentan towards Avranches on July 23, in hope of cutting off the American offensive. Both side suffered heavy losses. While fighting continued in northern France, the British finally begun their breakout of Greece. British commandos landed on the east coast of Greece near Larisa. Aid was given to Yugoslavian and Greek partisans who caused a great deal of disruption of German supply lines, helping to divert badly needed German troops from Greece to Yugoslavia.

# WAR IN THE PACIFIC, 1945

In the Pacific the Japanese were losing the war at a much faster rate than in our time line. The United States had devoted greater resources to the Pacific War. The American Navy bypassed tough island bases where the Japanese were dug in. General MacArthur insisted the United States conduct a campaign of island-hopping. MacArthur by passed the strongest Japanese-held islands and took only weakly held islands where the U. S. set up its own bases. By using both its surface and submarine fleets, the United States was able to dominate the Pacific and cut Japanese lines of supply, choking off the Japanese economy by denying the importation of badly needed resources from the Dutch East Indies and Southeast Asia. This policy also enabled the Americans to prevent the Japanese from reinforcing and supplying islands they held behind American lines.

The Americans captured the Volcanic Islands, including Iwo Jima, after several weeks of bloody fighting. The Americans suffered heavy casualties because the Japanese defended the island to the last man. But the capture of these islands permitted the Americans to begin around-the-clock air bombardment of Japanese cities with their B-29s. The B-29 could fly high enough to remain out of range of Japanese fighters defending the Japanese home islands. This meant the Americans could bomb Japan at will, causing horrible devastation to Japanese cities. Japanese cities were made of wood and paper and easily transformed into flaming infernos.

In Burma the British were able to push the Japanese back into Thailand. Aid began flowing into China and Chinese resistance by the nationalist forces toughened throughout the first half of 1945. American planes could now fly from the Philippines and Okinawa and land in China.

# THE SOVIET OFFENSIVE OF SUMMER 1945

The Soviet armies far outnumbered the Germans in 1945, but they had no where bear the level of technological and fighting ability as in our time line. The quality of the Soviet armies had improved but was still not equal to the Germans. The Soviet offensive of the Winter of 1944-45 inflicted heavy casualties on the Germans and their allies, but the Red Army also suffered high casualties. With Moscow still in German hands in 1945, the Soviet had to rely heavily on the vast numbers of American trucks for mobility. The Soviets were also now producing huge numbers of their T-34 tanks, but they were still not equal to the German panther and King Tiger tanks. But the Germans had suffered heavy losses and their losses exceeded their production of new tanks.

The Red Army was also suffering from casualties the Germans were inflicting on it. The Soviets were beginning to scrape the bottom of the barrel for its manpower needs, because most of the Russian heartland was totally or partially in German hands throughout the period of 1942 to 1945. Stalin now ordered all males, from thirteen to sixty-five years old to be drafted. The era of the Red Army absorbing millions of casualties was over.

The Soviets are still deep in their own territory in the Summer of 1945 and began to think about a separate peace with the Germans in hope of reclaiming then 1941 borders. With the British in Greece, Stalin feared the Anglo-Americans will capture the Balkans and might even try to restrict the U. S. S. R. to its 1939 borders after the war.

Before Roosevelt died, Stalin had over 300 Red spies within the Roosevelt administration, even holding high positions within FDR's cabinet. Stalin was receiving intelligence about the American Manhattan Project to build the Atomic Bomb. He knew that the Americans would have the Atomic bomb before 1946. With President Dewey in the White House, most of Stalin's spies had been replaced, and Stalin no longer trusted the Americans and the British. He hoped for one more major offensive to retake Moscow and then offer Hitler peace terms in return for the Soviet 1941 borders.

On June 13, Operation Kremlin opened with a short artillery bombardment, followed by infantry reconnaissance units, which used the cover of the artillery to move into attack positions. This was typical of Soviet operations under Marshal Zhukov. Zhukov next ordered a massive artillery assault against German lines all along Army Group Center within twenty-four hours. On June 14 heavy infantry swarmed across the lines towards the German positions. They were supported by dense formations of Soviet aircraft. This was followed by tank assaults which broke through the German defensive positions and cutting into the rear of the German armies.

The assault on the Moscow salient included 166 divisions and was supported by 2600 tanks and 1200 aircraft. Against this, Army Group Center, along a 800 mile front, possessed only 47 divisions, supported by 1100 tanks, mainly Tiger, King Tiger and Panther tanks, but the Germans were receiving large numbers of the He 162 jet fighters and some Me 262 jet fighters.

The first German army to suffer was the 9th, south of Moscow. It was threatened with encirclement until it retreated to the west of Moscow. It was ordered to hold open the road to Moscow and prevent the encirclement of Moscow. The 4th Army north of Moscow also suffered heavy casualties having to retreat back into Moscow. The 3rd Pz Army, located east of Moscow retreated and fought a mobile defense, inflicting heavy casualties on the advancing Red Army, but it could not keep the Soviets closing its pincers west of Moscow. Hitler was always had a phobia about Moscow, and now feared he would duplicate Napoleon's disastrous retreat of a century and a half earlier. He immediately ordered the withdrawal of the Moscow salient. The Germans were able to withdraw to a line running from Tikhvin in the north to Novgorod down to Smolensk and finally along the

Dneiper River. In the Southern most end of the Soviet offensive, the Red Army was able to take Kiev.

By July 27, the Soviet offensive slowed to a halt. Stalin offered Hitler his peace terms, but Hitler rejected a withdrawal to the 1941 borders. With the Allies, building out their forces in northern France, now breaking out of their Normandy beach head, and the British attacking in Greece, Hitler's generals pleaded with Hitler to cut a deal with the Soviet Union so they could drive the Anglo-Americans off the continent in France and Greece. Hitler finally agrees. On August 1, an armistice is signed between Germany and the Soviet Union. The Germans agree to withdraw to the 1939 Soviet borders. Hitler hopes to attack the Soviets once again, after he has defeated the Americans and the British. Stalin also plans to break the armistice once the Germans divert most of their forces to France and Greece.

# THE ALLIES DROP ATOMIC BOMBS ON HAMBURG AND HIROSHIMA

Both President Dewey and Prime Minister Churchill are furious at Stalin's betrayal. On July 16, 1945, the Americans successfully test the first Atomic bomb at Alamogrado, New Mexico. The United States produce two more A-bombs. Dewey met with Churchill and the two agreed that they would drop one of the bombs on Hamburg and the other on Hiroshima on July 6. They also agree that they would not seek unconditional surrender. Terms would be presented to both the Germans, Italians and the Japanese after the bombs are dropped. The two leaders then discuss the terms they would present to the Axis powers.

On July 6, two B-29 bombers took off on their deadly missions. One left an airfield in England heading for Hamburg, while the other left Tinian Island in the Marianas for Hiroshima. Both bombs were dropped causing massive devastation to both cities. Statements were immediately released from the White House to both Berlin and Tokyo. The statements call for an immediate cessation of hostilities, followed by the withdrawal of all occupied territories in Europe and the Far East. All German and Japanese forces were to return to their home countries. The Nationalist Socialist, Fascist and Imperial governments of Germany, Italy and Japan were to be removed. In Germany and Italy, the Allies were willing to talk with the Military authorities, while in Japan the Allies wanted to speak with civilian representatives of the Emperor. The only exception to Axis withdrawal was in Eastern Europe. The Germans and their allies, would agree to their armistice terms with the Soviet Union and withdraw to the Soviet 1939 borders. The

German military would permit the return of the Polish government in exile to Warsaw, as well as the governments of the three Baltic states, supporting them in restoring order to those countries. The Allies also warned that if the Axis powers refused this offer, they could expect further destruction on as great a level as Hamburg and Hiroshima. This was actually a buff, because the United States did not have any more Atomic bombs, and it would be months before they could produce additional weapons.

In Hitler's military headquarters in East Prussia, Hitler refused the Allied terms, but his generals, including Jodl and Keitel, both refuse to obey his orders. They understood the destructive power of the Atomic bomb and did not want to see Germany destroyed. Churchill and Dewey both having to abandon Roosevelt's "unconditional surrender" proposal are willing to negotiate a peace with Germany and Italy if National Socialist and Fascist governments are removed. It was the possibility of a negotiated peace with the Allies that convinced them they could save Germany and the German military. Even Goering sides with the generals. Hitler is trapped, but eventually agrees. However only under one condition—he askes his generals to permit him to commit suicide. The Allies want him and the other National Socialist leaders turned over as war criminals. The Generals agree and Hitler takes his life by putting a gun into his mouth, blowing his head off. Afterwards, Goering is made head of state and accepted the allied terms.

Many of the top National Socialists flee Germany. Himmler had tried to open his own negotiations with the Allies, but fails. He and Rosenberg finally flee to Sweden, while Goebbels, with his wife and children, flee to Spain. Mussolini also flee to Spain. Borman and many other Nazi leaders are able to flee to Switzerland. The military makes no effort to stop them for they fear that if they did, it might plunge Germany into civil war.

## JAPAN FIGHTS ON

The Japanese refused to accept the Allies' demands. The Japanese military was determined to fight on. They waited to see if the Allies would drop another such atomic bomb, but when another bomb was not dropped, the military convinces the Emperor to fight on.

When the Allies realized that Japan is not going to surrender, President Dewey agrees on two things: first, the United States would have to invade Japan, and second, another atomic bomb would have to be manufactured as soon as possible. On November 1, 1945, the United States invades the island of Kyushu. Americans land in the Kagoshima and Ariake Bay areas of southern Kyushu. The purpose was to gain naval and air bases for the final knock-out blow aimed at the industrial and political heart of Japan in the Tokyo-Yokohama area. The Japanese had assembled 5,000 Kamikaze and 3,000 conventional planes to repel the American invasion. The remainder of the Japanese fleet, including all of its submarines, were assembled to resist the invasion. The Japanese had organized a home defense army of 2,350,000 men and four million para-military fighters. The Americans suffered 35,000 dead and 85,000 injures, but the Japanese casualties were three times as great. By December 25, the southern half of the island is secured. Dewey receives word that the two additional atomic bombs would be available by March. The invasion of the main island of Japan is postponed.

Because of the Allies' refusal to permit the Soviets to occupy the territories that Stalin conquered in 1939-1940, Stalin refuse to attack Japan in August, 1945. Instead, he informs the Japanese that the Soviet Union would honor its non-aggression pact with Japan. This permits the Japanese to withdraw several divisions from Manchuria to reinforce the Japanese home islands.

On March 1, 1946 two additional atomic bombs are dropped on the cities of Nagasaki and Yokohama on March 6. On March 8, 1946 the Emperor of Japan announces over the radio that Japan will accept the Allied terms. General Tojo, as well as many other military leaders, in the tradition of Bushido, committed suicide.

# CONCLUSIONS

This scenario, I believe is very likely. If the Germans had concentrated their forces in 1942 on Moscow instead of the south, they would have had the decisive battle they were looking for. The Soviets were determined to defend Moscow with all available forces and would not have retreated as they did when the Germans attacked in Operation Blue. The Germans still had the forces necessary to achieve a victorious conclusion to attack Moscow. The fall of the Red Capital would not ensure the defeat of the Soviet Union, but it would have weakened the Red Army and pushed back its timetable of counter attacks for at least a year. The fall of Moscow and a tactical defeat of the Soviets in 1942 would also have put the Germans in a stronger position for 1943 and 1944.

The Allies would have been forced to move up the date for Operation Torch. In reality, FDR wanted the invasion of North Africa to begin in October, instead of November, so he could present the public with victory before the 1942 elections. So this is also a reasonable assumption. The Germans would still have lost the war but the end would have been very different. The defeat of Torch would have delayed the Anglo-American timetable for operations in the European Theater. Roosevelt wanted to concentrate on Europe, but a defeat in 1942 could have forced the United States to reallocate much of its resources to operations in the Pacific. There would have been no invasion of France in 1944 and relations between the Soviets and the Anglo-Americans would have been worst than in our time line. FDR was gravely ill in 1944 and he died during the first four months of 1945. If the war progressed at a much slower rate in our time line, it is very possible and even probable, that FDR would have died a year earlier. With Roosevelt out of the picture, the Democratic Party, which was already spilt (the Southerner Democrats often sided with the Republicans in both houses of the Congress), would have fractured with the leftist Henry Wallace as the Democratic candidate in 1944. If Thomas E. Dewey had been elected President, he would not have remained as committed to FDR's Unconditional Surrender policy. Even Churchill and Stalin disagreed with this policy, and Churchill could probably have convinced Dewey to have abandoned the policy. With the Germans still in control of most of Europe in the Summer of 1945, it is very possible that after the Allies dropped an A-bomb on a German city, the German High Command would have either forced Hitler to resign or removed him by force if the Allies assured them of reasonable terms.

In this time line, the Germans did not begin to lose the war until 1944, therefore the extermination programs could not begin until much later. Less than a million people were killed in the camps in this time line. After the war, the Hohenzollern monarchy, modeled after Great Britain's was put into place in Germany. Goering proved an able negotiator and was able to convince Dewey and Churchill that a strong Germany was still necessary in central Europe. Because of Stalin's treachery, the Allies, especially Churchill, agreed with Goering. Churchill did not want to repeat the failure of the Versailles Treaty. Germany was permitted to retain its 1938 borders, plus Austria. The Sudetanland was not returned to the Czechs. A strong German military was permitted, and Germany was allied to the United States, Great Britain and France against the Soviet Union.

In the Pacific, The Japanese would not surrender after only one atomic bomb. It would take the dropping of a second and even a third bomb before Japan surrendered. The invasion of Japan was bloody. Stalin's refusal to attack Japan was one of the first acts of the Cold War between the Soviet Union and the West.

When Japan finally surrendered, the Emperor was retained but the Japanese Imperial military establishment was removed. MacArthur was given the job of

# WHAT IF JAPAN WENT TO WAR IN 1940?

## BY
### ROBERT BLUMETTI

This is an improbable scenario, but an interesting one. It is based on the assumption that the Axis powers set-up a joint command and coordinated their strategies to a greater degree. This would result in a joint German-Italian High Command. The Germans would probably have decided to conduct a Mediterranean strategy in 1940-41, in order to drive the British out of the Mediterranean Sea and the Middle East. It would also have encouraged the Japanese to enter the war a year earlier, but this would have called for greater cooperation between the Japanese army and navy.

After Germany defeated Poland in September 1939, Hitler made several attempts to end the war by extending peace feelers to Britain. But British Prime Minister Chamberlain, distrusted Hitler after Germany broke the 1938 Munich agreement and occupied the remainder of the Czech state earlier that year, refused to consider any peace proposal. Hitler decided that Germany would have to move in the West and ordered his generals to come up with a plan for an attack on the Wets. The German generals kept postponing the invasion date because of bad weather. Hitler finally decided that the invasion of the West would have to be delayed until May of 1940.

During the Winter of 1939-1940, the Soviet Union invades Finland. The Finns put up an heroic fight but they were forced to surrender in March 1940.

The Soviets also occupy the three Baltic states. Germany gets wind of British plans to invade Norway and strike first. Norway and Denmark are occupied in March 1940. With their northern flank covered, Germany attacks the West in May. German Army Group B invades the Netherlands and Belgium. Franco-British forces invade Belgium to meet the Germans, But German Army Group A attacks through the Ardennes and out flanks the Allies. The Allies are split and forty divisions are either destroyed or captured, but the British are able to evacuate 330,000 troops at Dunkirk. Germany then turns south and overruns France. Italy declares war on France and Britain on June 10, 1940. Soon after France surrenders. Britain now stands alone against an Axis dominated Europe.

In June 1940 Hitler once again offers peace to Great Britain, but the newly appointed Prime Minister Churchill is determined to resist Germany. He hopes to hold out as long as he can, until President Roosevelt is able to bring the United States into the war. Roosevelt wants to enter the war, but the American people oppose going to war. Roosevelt decides to run for a third term in 1940 by campaigning on a promise to keep America out of the war in Europe, all the while he is secretly trying to maneuver the United States into the war.

# ADMIRAL RAEDER'S PLAN

Hitler is faced with a intransigent Britain and he must decide whether or not Germany will invade the British Isles. Hitler finally decides that it would be too difficult to try and cross the English Channel. Even if the Luftwaffe could secure air supremacy over the English Channel, they would still have to deal with the superior British Navy. Grand Admiral Raeder of the German Navy convinces Hitler that Operation Sea Lion is impossible and that the best course of action is to strike through the Mediterranean and the Middle East. He points our that the British are most vulnerable in the Mediterranean. He points out that Italy is not prepared for war. Unless Germany takes charge of the war in the Mediterranean Italy will be driven out of Africa, opening up the Balkans as a theater of war against Germany. He convinces Hitler that the Mediterranean question must be cleared up over the winter months, while German U-boats should conduct operations in the Atlantic as the Luftwaffe maintains pressure on the British Isles through bombing operations.

The German High Command draws up a plan of operation that will include taking Gibraltar and Malta, invading Egypt, the Suez Canal, an advance through Palestine and link up with Vichy Syria. Turkey and the entire Balkans will be forced to join the Axis. Next Iraq and Iran will be occupied and Britain will be drive out of the Persian Gulf. At the same time Germany should convince Japan to entire the war against Britain in the Far East. If Britain does surrenders by this time, German and Japanese forces could link up in India. This could be achieved by the summer of 1941. The Soviets will find themselves entirely surrounded by the Axis. Hitler agrees to the plan and rescinds his orders to demobilize a portion of the German army in the Summer of 1940.

## JAPAN PREPARES FOR WAR

The United States opposed Japan's war against China. In the summer of 1939 FDR ordered the slashing of Japan's oil futures. This was done by terminating the U.S. Treaty of Commerce with Japan at the end of a six-month notice. This meant the end of American oil, which both the Japanese army and navy were dependent on. After Britain and France declared war on Germany, Japanese militarists saw the possibility of expanding their empire to the south. Britain withdrew her gunboats from China. Both Britain and France began transferring their troops stationed in their Asian colonies to Europe. The only thing that stopped the militarists in the Japanese government from declaring war was the last of the moderates in Japan's General Abe's government. But Abe's government soon falls and is replaced by the Imperial Rule Assistance Association, founded by Former Prime Minister Konoye to prepare Japan for war. The IRAA begins to transform Japan into a Fascist society.

After Germany overruns Norway, Denmark, the Netherlands, Belgium and France, the militarist in Japan began to make plans to enter the war. Japan puts pressure on Britain to close the Burma Road to China. The British agrees, but after six months reopene it. The Japanese army agitates for Japan to join Germany and Italy in attacking Britain. In June 1940, Colonel Hashimoto leads a plot that kills the prime minister. The Japanese army seizes power. Konoye is made prime minister. Yosuke Matsuoka is made foreign minister and Hideki Tojo is war minister. Both are hawks. Japan allies itself with Germany and Italy. With France and the Netherlands defeated by Germany, Japan seeks to acquire their Asian colonies.

## HITLER MEETS WITH MUSSOLINI, PETAIN AND FRANCO

Over the Summer Hitler meets with Mussolini, informing him of plans for operations in the Mediterranean. At first Mussolini is reluctant to agree. He wants to conduct his own war, but Hitler is able to persuade him with promises of augmenting his New Roman Empire with the French Colony of Tunisia, Corsica, and Nice and Savoy. In the end Mussolini agrees to a joint German-Italian command, which the Germans will come to dominate. Hitler meets with Marshal Petain and informs him that German troops will pass through French territory. Petain protest to no avail. Hitler warns him that any opposition to German operations in the Mediterranean will result in the destruction of France. Petain quickly capitulates, hoping that for France will survive the war intact. Hitler next meets with Franco. Franco was convinced by the German traitor Admiral Canaris not to cooperate with Hitler, but when he meets with the Fuehrer he finds Hitler determined not to take no for an answer. When Franco makes exorbitant demands for Spain's cooperation, Hitler quickly agrees. He later tells Foreign Minister von Ribbentrop that he has no intension of letting Franco blackmail him, and will reward Spain with what he decides Spain deserves.

A conference is held by Hitler and the OKW in September 1940. Plans for Operation Sphinx are drawn up. The Army's Commander-in-Chief, Field Marshal Walter von Brauchitsch points out difficulties in the plans for operations in the Mediterranean. Yet, Hitler brushes aside Brauchitsch's objections to Reader's plans. Reports are given on the strength of the British Navy in the Mediterranean is divided between Gibralter and Alexandria. The Italian Navy's strength is also reviewed. The Germans are confident that the British Navy will not be able to prevent a combined Spanish-German assault on Gibralter. The British only have 50,000 troops spread throughout North Africa and the Middle East, with 36,000 and one armor division in Egypt. The Italians have 200,000 troops in East Africa and 250,000 in Libya, but the Italian army is not prepared for an offensive. It is agreed that four Panzer divisions under Erwin Rommel, who is to be promoted, should be sent to Libya. It is also agreed that two German Air Fleets should be transferred to the Mediterranean, and combined with the Italian air forces. The Axis are able to dominate the skies above the entire theater operating from bases in Spain, the Balearics, Sardinia, Italy, Sicily, Libya and ultimately Egypt.

# HITLER MEETS WITH JAPAN'S FOREIGN MINISTER, OSHIMA

Hitler now meets with the Japanese Ambassador to Germany, Lieutenant General Oshima Hiroshi. Hitler confides to him to an unprecedented degree. Oshima is moved by Hitler's candidacy. Hitler proposes that Japan should attack Britain in the Far East. Japan could then occupy the Dutch East Indies, and conquer British possessions in South East Asia and China. Once the Germans have occupied the Middle East and Japan conquers Burma, the Axis could link-up in Southern Asia. India will be at their mercy and the Japanese Fleet could dominate the Indian Ocean. By the time their meeting ends, there is little that Oshima doesn't know about German plans.

Oshima quickly wires the results of his meeting to Tokyo. The Japanese high command is divided on what course of action Japan should take. The Army wants to concentrate on land ventures either in China or against the Soviet Union. The Navy wants to concentrate on naval actions, but is undecided whether they should prepare for a future war with the United States or strike south against British and Dutch colonies. Oshima's main opponent is General Tojo. There was some talk about occupying French Indochina. Tojo wanted to make peace with the Soviet Union and prepare for an attack on the United States, but other naval officers thought it wiser to strike at the British and Dutch colonies. With the Germans and Italians concentrating in driving the British out of the Mediterranean and the Middle East, it is believed that Japan has a golden opportunity to occupy the British and Dutch colonies before the United States could possibly intervene. Tojo still thought it was necessary to include the United States in a Japanese attack, but Admiral Isoroku Yamamoto opposed an attack on the United States. Finally, after much debate, the "Southern Strategy" faction within the Japanese Navy forms an alliance with the Japanese Army leader. They are able to convince the high command that the best course of action is to accept Hitler's plan for a joint Axis attack against British positions in the Middle East, Southern Asia and the Indian Ocean. It is agreed that there should be no attack on the Americans. The Japanese began planning an attack on the British and Dutch possessions by attacking the British naval base at Singapore on Sunday morning, December 6, 1940.

# THE POSITION OF THE UNITED STATES IN 1940

The British had been successful in breaking both the Japanese and German military codes. When they learned that the Japanese were preparing for some kind of attack against them, Churchill immediately contacts Roosevelt. He wanted FDR to put pressure of Japan, even threaten to go to war against to Japan if Japan attacks Britain or the Dutch colonies in the Far East. But Roosevelt is unable to do anything. He was too busy trying to get reelected. His campaign was built around lies that he wanted to keep the United States out of the war. The United

States was not yet ready to confront Japan. The Americans would need at least another year to build up their forces. Unless the Japanese attacked the United States, the Congress would never declare war because the 80% of the American people still oppose the United States going to war. If Japan attacks Britain in 1940, Britain would have to stand alone.

# ATTACK ON GIBRALTER

On November 8 German and Spanish guns open fire from across Algeciras Bay on the fortress of Gibralter. The British could do little to retaliate. Their guns were far inferior to the German and Spanish guns. The British Navy responds with an attack on the Spanish Fleet at Cadiz. The Spanish Fleet is badly damaged. Gibralter holds out for three weeks, but finally surrenders on November 30 after a Spanish infantry assault supported by the Luftwaffe. The Western Mediterranean is cut off to the British.

# ATTACK ON MALTA

The fall of Gibralter is quickly followed by an assault on the island of Malta. On November 25 the Italian Admiral Inigo Campiori leads the Italian Battle Fleet into the Mediterranean with orders to confront the British Mediterranean Fleet under Admiral Cunningham. The Axis High Command hoped this would provide cover for a paratroop assault on Malta targeted for November 28 and 29. Two German panzer groups, Pzkw II and Pzkw III, are fitted for an amphibious landing on the coast of the island after the paratroops captured the two airfields.

The Italian and British fleet met each other on November 29, in the Ionian Sea. The Italians had the greater number of ships, but the British had stronger battleships. The battle was fierce and the Italians fought heroically, but were no match for the British. But the British did suffer heavy damage to several ships, including its battleship Illustrious. Admiral Cunningham realized that he could not get the upper hand over the Italians. The battle was now moving within range of the German and Italian air patrols. Cunningham realized that he would have to break off the battle and return to Alexandra, in Egypt, because his ships were now within range of Axis airplanes.

The German airborne invasion of Malta almost fails, but because of British mistakes, the Germans are able to capture one of the airfields in the first day of the invasion. Fighting continues for several days over the second airfield, but air support from German and Italian fighters and Stuka bombers give the Germans the upper hand. By December 3 the second airfield falls to the Germans. While the fighting for the airfields continues, one German and two Italian infantry divisions began landing on the coast of Malta under fire support from two Italian battleships. German tanks soon come ashore and join the fighting. The British put up stiff resistance, but they were outnumbered and outgunned. By December 12, the island is firmly in the hands of the Germans and the Italians.

# BRITISH WITHDRAWAL FROM THE MEDITERRANEAN

General Wavell realized that the British could not stop the advance of the Axis from overrunning Egypt and the entire Middle East with the forces available. He decided that the best plan is to withdraw from Egypt, Palestine and Jordan and take a stand in the Persian Gulf. He wants what was left of the British Fleet to withdraw to the Red Sea and bomb up the Suez Canal. Churchill vetoes this plan. He wanted Wavell to attack Libya and drive the Italians from North Africa before the Germans reinforce the Italians. But Wavell opposes this plan. He knew that the Germans were arriving in Tripoli and would soon join the Italians stalled at Sidi Barrani. Churchill finally relents and Wavell begins withdrawing from Egypt. Some of his forces began moving up the Nile, hoping to hold the Sudan and eventually join a planned invasion of Italian East Africa. But most of the British force withdrew to Iraq and dig into a fortified defensive position around the oil rich region around Basra.

# JAPANESE DECLARES WAR ON THE BRITISH EMPIRE

On October 31, 1940, the Japanese hit British air and naval forces throughout southeast Asia. The U.S. Presidential elections are scheduled for November 3. The Japanese knew that President Roosevelt could not react to Japanese aggression against the British and the Dutch in the Far East without endangering his chances of reelection. The American people did not want to go to war, so long as the Japanese bypassed American territories in the Far East. FDR would not risk the anger of the American public by interfering with Japan entering the war on Germany's side. Japanese forces bypassed the Phillipines and all other U.S. territories, heading for Malaya, Singapore and Hong Kong. The British had long ago learned of an impending attack by Japan and were on alert. The Japanese fleet was spotted heading south into the South China Sea. Over 200,000 Japanese shock troops were permitted to land in Vichy-controlled Indo-China and Thailand. On October 31, the Japanese swarmed against the British and Dutch appearing with overwhelming strength at critical fighting points. The way for conquest was smoothed by fifth columns in each of the areas selected for infiltration or assault.

The British had regarded Singapore as their strongest naval base in the Empire. It was suppose to be impregnable and might have been from the sea, but the Japanese struck from the mainland. Japan wanted the huge supply of tin and rubber in the Malaya Peninsula. They sent 200,000 specially trained jungle fighters to take Southeast Asia. General Tomoyuki Yamashita's 25th army landed on the peninsula at Singora and moved toward Kra. Additional Japanese troops began moving south from Thailand toward Singapore. In the Middle of November 1940, the British, outwitted and demoralized, staggered back down the length of the peninsula to Singapore. The British rushed in some reinforcements, but it was too little, too late. On November 18, 1941, Lieutenant General Sir Arthur Ernest Percival surrendered over 50,000 British troops. It was the most humiliating defeat the British ever suffered.

The Japanese began bombing Hong Kong for two weeks, and then on November 17 Japanese troops land, quickly cuttin off the water supply. The British garrison of 11,000 troops finally surrender on Christmas day. The British fleet had sailed out of Singapore to confront the Japanese fleet in the South China sea, but they didn't take into consideration Japanese bombers. They approached the British fleet from 10,000 feet and assaulted the British fleet with consummate skill and determination with both high-level bombing and torpedo attacks. The British fleet was destroyed. The way was now open for the Japanese to assault British and Dutch colonies throughout southeastern Asia and in the Indian Ocean.

The Japanese now turned south to the Dutch East Indies. Java was the most important island, rich in rice, quinine, oil and manganese. It was defended by an unreliable native force of just 10,000, and a small Dutch fleet. On November 23, 1940, a small Japanese force landed at Luching and at four other locations two weeks later: Bantan, Indramayu, Rembang, and Java. A week later another force storme ashore at Brunei and British North Borneo, capturing the oil fields located there. The Japanese also attack the northern coast of New Guinea and Ronaud in New Britain. The Dutch fleet and several British ships led by Dutch Admiral Helfrich are overwhelmed by superior Japanese firepower and numbers. On February 1, 1941, all of the Dutch East Indies finally surrender to Japan, and 98,000 troops are captured.

From Thailand, the Japanese next invade Burma. Their invasion is synchronized with their assault on Malaya. The main strike came on December 11, 1940. Powerful Japanese shock troops infiltrate through the jungles and in two weeks captured Moulmein, opposite Rangoon, in the Gulf of Martaban. A second Japanese force push through Northern Burma toward Rangoon and Lashio. By the end of March, the British are driven out of Burma and forced back into India.

# ROMMEL'S ADVANCE TO THE PERSIAN GULF

On December 15 1940, Rommel races across Libya from Tripoli to join the Italians waiting at Sidi Barrani. On December 23 Rommel reaches El Alamen and continues on to Cairo. On Christmas Day elements of the Egyptian army, led by two colonels, Gamal Abdel Nassar and Anwar el Sadat. Mussolini flies down to Egypt and joines the Italian and German troops that entered Cairo. He is welcomed by Colonel Nassar and Colonel Sasat and declares Egypt a protectorate and under Italian and German supervision. Rommel didn't wait to celebrate. He races toward the Suez Canal where he confronts 30,000 British and Commonwealth troops before they could blow up the canal and withdraw. The British resists, but are unable to stop Rommel's three panzer divisions. Only five thousand Commonwealth troops are able to escape, but they did blow up a section of the canal before they leave. Rommel also sends one panzer division with two Italian divisions up the Nile to link up with the Italians in Italian East Africa. The Italians struck north from Ethiopia and the British were cut off from any escape. They tried to reach the Red Sea coast, but failed. Five thousand Commonwealth troops surrenders Atbara in the Sudan. Cunningham is ordered to sail for Ceylon in case the Japanese decides to attack India.

Rommel now enters Palestine. He is accompanied by the Grand Mufti, the leader of the Palestinian Arabs who had fled to Germany. The Grand Mufti broadcasts over the radio, pleading for the Arab population to rise up against the British and welcome the Germans as liberators. Rommel enters Jerusalem on January 21, 1941. He was welcomed by the Arabic population. Many Arabs began attacking and killing Jews. Zionist terrorist groups, flee with the British to Iraq. The pro-Axis Vichy government in Syria permits the Germans to land fighters and bombers on airbases in Syria. The Luftwaffe begins attacking the British in Iraq. When Rommel enters Iraq on February 16, 1941, the Iraqis rebels and welcomes the Germans as liberators. On February 26 Rommel attacks the British position around Basara. Fighting continues for five days, but it soon becomes obvious that the British could not stop the Germans from breaking through. On March 3, the British withdrew from Iraq, sailing for India.

# THE BRITISH SURRENDER

With nothing standing in their way the Japanese attack both India and Australia, with the Germans entering Iran, with the Iranians welcoming them as liberators, the British Parliament decides to sue for peace. A vote of no confidence brings the Churchill government down, and Churchill boarded a ship for Canada. Halifax is asked to set up a new government. President Roosevelt wires Halifax, encouraging him to stay in the war. But when Halifax asks Roosevelt if the United States will enter the war on Britain side, Roosevelt declines. On March 3, 1941, the British government asks the governments of Germany, Italy and Japan for an armistice. The Second World War had come to an end.

With the defeat of Britain, a peace conference is held in Munich. Great Britain loses all her possessions in the Mediterranean, North Africa and the Middle East. South Africa is given its independence and joins the Axis. The Afrikaners who dominate South Africa establish a Nazi-like government. Britain and France turn over to Germany the former German colonies in Africa that were taken from her at Versailles. Japan annexes British possessions in Southeast Asia, including Burma. India remains British, but the Indian Congress Party begins demonstrating for Indian independence. Japan also annexes French Indo-China and the Dutch East Indies. The Germans agrees to withdraw from most of France, but annexes not only Alsace-Lorraine but also a strip of territory running from Geneva to the mouth of the Somme river on the English Channel. Belgium, Luxembourg and the Netherlands are all annexed to Greater Germany. The French retains Algeria and Syria, but Italy annexes Tunisia, Corsica, Nice and Savoy, and Spain annexes Morocco. The British also have to withdraw from Egypt, Somiland, Palestine, Jordan, Iraq, Iran, Sudan and Kenya. The last two are annexed by Italy, while the rest are occupied by German and Italian troops and given native governments allied to both powers.

The British and French empires are devastated. Both countries agrees to join Hitler's New Order allying themselves to Germany. Canada, Australia and New Zealand all leave the British Empire seeking an alliance with the United States. Roosevelt sends Secretary Hull to draw up treaties of alliances with all three countries. There is opposition in Congress, but Roosevelt appealed to the American people, calling for solidarity with these three English-speaking cousins of the United States. Public opinion is still against the United States going to war, but the expansion of Japan into large sections of Southeast Asia frightens many Americans into supporting Roosevelt's treaties. The treaties were passed and Canada, Australia and New Zealand were now allied to the United States.

# THE JAPANESE DEBATE THE FUTURE OF JAPANESE EXPANSION.

The Japanese high command was still divided on the future course of Japanese expansion. With the annexation of British, French and Dutch colonies in Southeast Asia, Japan now possessed the necessary mineral resources needed to survive an American economic embargo. Roosevelt's embargo becomes meaningless. But Roosevelt is able to pass bills that expanded the size of the United States Pacific Fleet. With the end of the war in Europe Roosevelt's plans to go to war against Nazi Germany are now dead. His desire to bring America into the war against Germany by forcing a conflict with her ally, Japan, leaves the United States in a terrible position of being isolated in a hostile world. Germany is hostile, Britain and France are defeated, FDR has alienated the Japanese by placing an embargo on Japan in the Summer of 1940. The only country left for the United States to form an alliance with is the Soviet Union, but Stalin is suspicious of the capitalist United States and there is too much opposition within the United States against such an alliance.

The Japanese military leaders understand this. Oshima, the foreign embassador to Germany, is told by Hitler that Germany was planning to go to war against the Soviet Union. He welcomes a Japanese attack on the Soviets in Siberia. The Japanese Army supports this plan. Jealous of the glory that the Japanese Navy won in its rapid victories in Southeast Asia, the Japanese Generals wants the opportunity for the Army to share in the glory. But there were still leaders among the Japanese Navy and government that feared the United States. Led by Tojo, this faction support preparing for a possible war against the United States in 1942 if the Americans continue to build-up their forces in the Pacific, especially in the Philippines. This worries the Japanese Navy. Admiral Yamamoto fears the American threat and believes war with the United States is inevitable, but he feels that war will not break out for at least another year. He decides to support the Army is plans for an attack on the Soviet Union if the Army will support a build-up of Naval forces for a future war with the United States after s Soviet defeat.

# GERMANY ATTACKS THE SOVIET UNION

When Hitler agrees to a Mediterranean strategy he orders the German economy to go on a total war footing in the Summer of 1940. It is necessary to build-up the German army and air force if Germany is going to have a military force strong enough to invade the Soviet Union in the Spring of 1941, while conquering the Mediterranean and the Middle East. In January 1941, Soviet Foreign Minister Molotov meets with Hitler. Hitler tries to convince Molotov that the Soviet Union should attack the British in Persia and India. Molotov ignores Hitler's proposals and presents Hitler with a list of demands: Finland, Yugoslavia, Bulgaria and Turkey are to come under the Soviet sphere of influence and all German troops are to withdraw from these countries as well as Romania. Hitler refuses Molotov's demands outright and the meeting breaks-up without any agreement. After Molotov returns to the Soviet Union, Hitler orders the German High Command to prepare for the invasion of the Soviet Union as soon as Britain is defeated. It is agreed that the invasion of the Soviet Union will commence on May 15, 1941. Hitler meets with the Japanese ambassador, suggesting that Oshima return to Japan and convince the Japanese government to join Germany in attacking the Soviets after the British are defeated. In the next few months the Germans convinced the Bulgarians, the Yugoslavs, the Greeks and the Turks to join the Axis along with the Romanians and the Hungarians.

On May 15 the Germans attacks the Soviet Union with 175 divisions and 75 allied divisions that included the Finns, the Romanians, the Hungarians, the Italians, the Spanish, the French and the Turks. The Axis forces are divided into four main fronts: Army group North attacks in the Baltic and plans to link up with the Finns east of Leningrad, Army Group Center attacks along the Minsk-Smolensk road toward Moscow, Army Group South attacks through the Ukraine while Army Group East attacked the Soviets in the Caucasus from Iran and Turkey. The Germans and their allies rapidly overwhelms the Soviets, capturing over two million prisoners of war and capturing Kiev and Leningrad by July. After securing the Ukraine and the Caucasus, the Germans turned on Moscow in August.

The Soviet's were running low on supplies. Roosevelt asks Congress to lend-lease aid to the Soviet Union, but strong opposition by right-wingers and anti-communists in Congress defeats Soviet lend-lease. The Soviets found it difficult to continue resisting the Germans. When the Germans attacks Moscow, Soviet resistance begins to crumble.

It had been Tojo's desire for many years to attack the Soviet Union. He felt Japan's humiliation when the United States and Britain forced Japan to evacuate Siberia after the First World War. Tojo planned the invasion of the Soviet Union when he was in charge of the Kwantung in Manchuria. Now the opportunity to carry out his invasion presented itself. The Japanese decided it was time to enter the war, attacking the Soviet Union on September 1. The Japanese quickly occupy Vladivostok, Khabarovsk and northern Sakhalin Island. The Soviets are able to slow down Japanese forces, but by October 20 the Japanese army success-fully invades Mongolia, reaching Nerchinsk, and occupying the Maritime Prov-ince. The Soviets could not relocate badly needed reserves from Siberia to the defense of Moscow because of the Japanese invasion of Siberia. Moscow is then surrounded by the Germans on September 15. Stalin and the Soviet government flee to Gorsky. Soviet citizens began rebelling against Soviet authorities. The Soviet military decides that they should sue for peace. When Stalin refuses he is killed by General Khukov. Khukov made contact with the Axis powers and agrees to an armistice. Soviet forces begins withdrawing to the Ural Mountains in the west, and withdraw from Mongolia and west of Lake Baykal in the East.

# THE RISE OF THE AMERICA FIRST MOVEMENT

In 1940 a collection of pacifists, socialists, conservatives, populists and pro-Ger-man elements joined together to form the America First Committee. The AFC was led by the aviation hero Charles Lindbergh. He campaigns hard throughout 1941 to keep America from going to war and seeks peace with Germany. With the defeat of Britain, the AFC became the strongest force in American politics. The AFC was able to dominate Congress and stop Roosevelt's plans to give led-lease aid to the Soviets. With the Axis powers now dominating the Euro-Asian landmass and Africa, Japan is able to receive all the resources it needs without relying on the United States. The Republicans claim that Roosevelt's policies were only alienating the Japanese and hurting American businesses by maintaining the embargo. In 1942, the AFC is able to get the Congress to lift the embargo on Japan.

Roosevelt's popularity rapidly declines and Lindbergh support increases. FDR's coalition in Congress crumbles. Southern segregationists withdraw sup-port for Roosevelt. The Republicans began pushing for Lindbergh to run for President in 1944 against Roosevelt. After the mid-tern elections of 1942, the

Republicans are able to recapture control of the House and the Democrats loose support in the Senate.

During the next year Roosevelt grows progressively ill. By the beginning of 1943 Roosevelt can only work a twenty-hour week. In March he suffers a stroke and Henry Wallace is made the acting President. On April 17, 1943, Roosevelt suffers a second stroke and dies. Wallace becomes President. Because of Wallace's leftist views and support for the New Deal, American politics becomes even more partisan than it was during the last twelve years. The Democratic Party rapidly loses support across the country.

With the end of the embargo against Japan, Japanese plans to attack the United States are postpone. The Japanese watch developments in the United States quite closely. Japanese Prime Minister, Tojo, invites Lindbergh to visit Japan in September, 1942. Lindbergh accepts the invitation is being warmly welcomed by the Japanese. When Lindbergh returns to the United States, he begins speaking across the United States warning about Roosevelt's plans to involve America in a war with Germany and Japan. With 90 percent of the American pubic solidly against war and behind Lindbergh, tensions between the United States and Japan lessens in the next few years. With the death of Roosevelt, Lindbergh quickly becomes the opposition leader to the left-leaning President Wallace. Support for Lindbergh continues to grow.

In 1944 Lindbergh is nominated as the Republican candidate for President, while the Democratic Party nominates President Henry Wallace. Lindbergh wins the election in a massive landside with 73 percent of the popular vote and every electoral vote.

# THE STATE OF THE WORLD IN 1945

In 1945 the world was a very different place than it was in 1939. Germany dominated Europe as far east as the Ural mountains. Germany also supported the British, French, the Spanish, the Portugese and the Italians in maintaining control of their empires in Africa, the Middle East and southern Asia. Japan controlled eastern Siberia, most of China, southeast Asia, Indonesia, and most of the western half of the Pacific ocean.

The United States was allied to Canada, Australia, New Zealand, controlled the eastern half of the Pacific ocean and dominated the entire Western Hemisphere. American society was deeply divided between left and right. With the withdrawal of the Southern conservatives from the Democratic party, the party was captured by the left as led by Henry Wallace. The Democratic Party soon became a minority party. The States' Rights Party was created by the Southern Democrats and allied itself with the Republican party. The GOP was dominated by an alliance of two factions; the conservative populists led by Robert Taft and Charles Lindbergh and corporate America who sought closer economic ties with Germany and Japan.

What was left of the former Soviet Union was now the Russian Federation and restricted to western Siberia and central Asia, controlling about forty million people. The Nationalist Chinese retreat to Tibet while the Chinese Communists retreat to Sinkiang, where the two forces continued the civil war unnoticed by the rest of the world.

0-595-30139-8

Printed in the United States
22158LVS00005B/31-39